D0130557

Award-winning author Anthony Masters knows how 'to hook his reader from the first page' *Books for Keeps*.

Anthony has written extensively for young adults and is renowned for tackling serious issues through gripping stories. He also writes for adults, both fiction and non-fiction. For the Orchard Black Apple list he has written the *Ghosthunter* series, the *Dark Diaries* series and four novels: *Spinner, Wicked, The Drop* and *Day of the Dead*, which was shortlisted for the Angus Award. He lives in Sussex with his wife and has three children.

Anthony Masters also runs *Book Explosions*, children's adventure workshops that inspire adrenalin and confidence in children, so that they can do their own creative writing.

Also by Anthony Masters

Dark Diaries

DEAD RINGER
FIRE STARTER
DEATH DAY
SHOCK WAVES

DAY OF THE DEAD
WICKED
THE DROP

Ghosthunters

DANCING WITH THE DEAD
DARK TOWER
DEADLY GAMES

Predator

SHARK ATTACK
HUNTED
DEATHTRAP

killer instinct

ANTHONY MASTERS

ORCHARD BOOKS

EAST SUSSEX SCHOOLS LIBRARY SERVICE	
09-Oct-03	PETERS
968037	

ORCHARD BOOKS
96 Leonard Street, London EC2A 4XD
Orchard Books Australia
32/45-51 Huntley Street, Alexandria, NSW 2015
ISBN 1 84121 908 8
First published in Great Britain in 2003
A paperback original
Text © Anthony Masters 2003
The right of Anthony Masters to be identified as the author
of this work has been asserted by him in accordance with
the Copyright, Designs and Patents Act, 1988.
A CIP catalogue record for this book is available from
the British Library.
1 3 5 7 9 10 8 6 4 2
Printed in Great Britain

Contents

For Sarah Dudman

PROLOGUE

In the time when the Dendid created all things,
He created the sun,
And the sun is born, and dies, and comes again.
He created the moon,
And the moon is born, and dies, and comes again;
He created the stars,
And the stars are born, and die, and come again;
He created man,
And man is born, and dies, and does not come again.

Based on an old Dinka tribal song.
Included in *The Unwritten Song*, ed. Willard Trask
(Cape, 1969)

Accident!

The late afternoon heat was still unbearable and to Tom the dusty grasslands seemed endless, an unchanging eternal landscape with the occasional clump of ancient stunted trees. Then, in the distance, he saw foothills, and breathing a sigh of relief returned to the argument he was having with his older brother Josh.

Arno, their guide, was trying not to listen to their quarrelling, keeping his eyes on the uneven track. He was only six years older than Josh, but had become their parents' much-trusted guide during the family's "holiday of a lifetime" in Kenya.

The jeep rocked as Arno attempted to avoid the potholes, while his dog, Ska, a large mongrel who looked like an elongated Alsatian, sat next to Tom in the back, swaying with the movement.

Josh was in the front, hat pulled well down over his eyes, and Tom could see the sweat running down his thick neck. They hadn't been getting on for well over a year now. Tom at thirteen, tall and skinny, had been teasing his brother about carrying too much weight. Josh was fifteen and his face was puffy, lips cracked. His lank, straw-like hair straggled from under his hat, falling damply on to his shoulders.

"You should do some circuit training," said Tom. "Get rid of that paunch."

"It's all muscle," Josh sneered. "*You* look like you've just come out of a refugee camp." Then he paused, remembering that Arno had been a refugee himself, crossing the border into Kenya from Uganda, leaving his family behind, eventually getting work as a guide and "now knowing the bush better than the locals", as Dad had told them.

"You're so gross." Tom was stung by his brother's insensitivity to Arno's feelings. "What are you? Just so gross."

Always short-tempered, Josh suddenly lost his cool, and bunching his fist he turned and leant over the back of the passenger seat to hit out at his brother.

Tom dodged and Josh punched the air, losing his balance. His whole solid bodyweight lurched into Arno just as the jeep hit a large pothole.

"Get off me!" Arno yelled, grappling for control of the steering. But their guide had hardly got the words out before the jeep veered off the track and skidded sharply into a gully, colliding head-on with the trunk of a tree, then bounced away and rolled over on to its side.

Clouds of choking dust rose and thickened. Slowly, Tom realised he had been thrown out of his seat. He was face-down on the baked, sandy soil, spluttering, eyes smarting.

For a while he lay there, too dazed to move, watching the swirling clouds of dust slowly clear. Then Tom heard a groaning sound and felt a surge of panic. Someone was hurt. Maybe badly. What an irresponsible idiot Josh was!

Tom sat up, mouth as dry as the dust, heart hammering. He couldn't see anything for a moment. Then, with huge relief, he heard Arno's voice.

"Tom, are you all right?" Arno's voice was sharp with anxiety. Short, sturdy and muscular, he radiated authority. But how would he be able to look after them now? thought Tom as he scrambled to his feet and stared at their guide in dismay. Tom and Josh's arguments had caused trouble before — broken windows, hurt feelings, their parents' anger. But this time, they had brought their feud to the wilderness with disastrous results.

"I think so. More than can be said for the jeep," replied Tom.

The vehicle was a shattered wreck, lying on its side with its bonnet stoved in, water streaming from the radiator and a wheel torn off, now some distance away at the back of the gully. Then Tom and Arno heard a groan of pain.

"Where's Josh?" Arno looked frantically around while Ska, who must have leapt clear of the jeep, jumped around them, unhurt.

The low moaning continued.

"Over here!" Arno was already on the other side of the wreck and Tom ran to join him, finding Josh lying on his back, one leg trapped under the overturned vehicle. His face was white, covered in sweat, lips twisted in pain. "We'll have to get the jeep off him," said Arno decisively, muscles bulging as he grabbed the buckled side. "You pull him out." Then seeing Tom's look of despair he added, "He'll be OK. The weight isn't entirely resting on his leg. The jeep's overturned at an angle."

The sweat poured down Arno's brow as he struggled to lift the side of the vehicle, his muscles knotted as he raised the wreckage by at least half a metre.

Amazed by Arno's display of strength, Tom grabbed Josh's shoulders and dragged him away while his brother howled with pain.

"He's clear."

His breath coming in short gasps, Arno let go and the jeep fell back on to its side with a thud.

Tom looked down at his brother's leg which was bent at a strange angle. He felt sick and then *was* sick, turning away from Josh, shoulders heaving, the vomit spreading over the dry grass.

Josh was still moaning in pain as Arno came over and knelt down, checking him out carefully.

"What's hurting?" Tom asked, and then stopped, knowing how stupid he must sound.

"My leg, you idiot!"

"You're lucky," Arno pronounced. "Your leg could easily have been crushed. As it is, I think you've only got a bad break."

"I don't feel lucky," said Josh.

Arno lifted the sleeping bags from the back of the jeep, and Tom helped him to fold them into pillows and unzip one as a cover for Josh. Josh, looking worn out, closed his eyes as if to sleep and Arno and Tom moved a few metres further away.

"What are we going to do?" asked Tom helplessly. "Where *are* we?"

"About nineteen miles from Matendu. It's in the foothills of Mount Elgon," said Arno. "But that's only a small settlement. There's a tribe – the Kala – who live there. But they've deliberately cut themselves off and I don't know what communications they have with the outside world. I don't even know if they've got a radio, but we can try to get in touch with them anyway." Ska was licking at Arno, and then transferred his attentions to Josh, who pushed the dog away.

"What are we going to do if they can't help us?" demanded Tom.

"We'll have to think again," replied Arno enigmatically, increasing Tom's anxiety.

Arno went back to the jeep. He leant cautiously through the broken window, and reached into the front compartment. Not finding what he wanted, he carefully stretched across the steering wheel, pulled out a map from the side pocket, but then continued to search. For the first time since he had met Arno, Tom heard him swear and saw that he was now checking around the outside of the jeep. Arno swore again and held up what was left of the radio. "Like my jeep, it's a write-off. Josh just escaped being crushed, but the radio didn't." He sounded bitter and at a loss.

"Are you insured?" asked Tom. Then he felt ridiculous, as if he was talking about a collision on a safe suburban road. But it was the safe suburban road that he craved. Then a sudden thought came to him and Tom gave a whoop of joy. "I've got a mobile!" He dragged it out of his pocket and began to punch in numbers, but he couldn't get a connection. "Can't be a signal here," he said despondently.

"I thought you'd got a pocket radio." Arno looked hopeful.

"I have, but it's smashed. I must have landed on it."

Arno's face fell and he stared at the horizon. The foothills were bathed in hard-edged sunlight and there was a herd of antelope grazing on the plain, bodies shimmering in the heat. There were zebra too, feeding on the dry grass, as Arno had told them a few minutes before the crash. The temperature was cooler and when Tom glanced down at his watch he saw it was now just before seven pm.

"What are we going to do?" Tom asked again.

"Camp here for the night. What else *can* we do? If only you guys had some control this wouldn't have happened." Arno sounded contemptuous. Tom felt angry. Josh was the one who'd been behaving like a kid, and had put them all at risk, not him.

Then, very suddenly, the sun went down. There was no twilight; it was as if a dark blanket had been thrown over the light.

"Why does the sun go down so fast?" asked Tom. He'd noticed the phenomenon before, but hadn't been curious enough to ask. Now, out here on the plain, the sun's sudden departure was much more obvious.

"It's because we're on the Equator," replied Arno. "The sun goes down at seven pm all the year round."

Snapped into darkness, Tom felt a wave of fear which he tried to control.

"Let's take a look at Josh," said Arno.

He appeared to be sleeping. Tom and Arno stood over him. Arno was looking at him carefully, apparently satisfied.

"Should he be asleep?" asked Tom.

"Yes – the pain will have exhausted him. He'll be fine."

"You're sure?"

"I'm not sure about anything," snapped Arno. "But I'll make Josh as comfortable as I can and in the morning I'll hike to Matendu. I hope to God the Kala *have* got a radio because, if not—" Arno paused.

"If not?" prompted Tom, the anxiety rising from the pit of his stomach.

"I'll have to try to reach Osak. Once we've sorted Josh out anyway." He picked up the map and studied it carefully. "They've got a landing strip, but it's a long way away from here. Thirty miles. Maybe more."

Tom felt an overwhelming sense of inadequacy and a creeping fear. This was the African grasslands – lion country. Before the accident they had been hoping to spot a pride from the safety of the jeep. But now the jeep wasn't safe any longer and neither were they.

During their visit to Kenya, Tom, Josh and their parents, Alan and Liz Trent, had already seen elephants, buffalo, monkeys and other wild animals, but they hadn't as yet sighted lion. Then, just as they were about to go on the best trip of the holiday, a five-day tour "lion hunting" including two days' camping at the end, Dad had picked up a tummy bug and Mum had elected to stay with him in the hotel.

"You go with Arno," Dad had said. "You can't come to Africa without seeing a lion. Arno's absolutely reliable and, who knows, you might get a lion in your lens." Dad had been talking about Josh's new video camera which was now somewhere in the wreck of the jeep – presumably smashed like the radios.

Tom turned to Arno who was still bending over the map.

"I'm sorry," said Tom.

"Mmm?" Arno was engrossed.

"The crash was our fault. Josh's always determined to have an argument. But this was one too many." Tom paused and then asked, "Why can't we make it to the Kala at Matendu tonight?"

Arno sighed and then made eye contact with Tom for the first time since the crash. He spoke slowly and patiently. "Because it's too dangerous to wander about after dark. I've told you about all the wild animals we could encounter already. So we're stranded until tomorrow morning. When we don't arrive at Kisimu on Wednesday evening, your parents will report us missing and the helicopter will come looking for us. I'll try the Kala before then in any case." Arno called to Ska, who came loping across obediently. But Tom thought he could see fear in the dog's eyes. Arno stroked Ska affectionately and then went back to the jeep again. "I'll try and get him a bowl of water."

Tom suddenly realised how thirsty *he* was – and what about Josh? Then he heard Arno give a muffled cry and

Tom could hardly bring himself to ask what was wrong.

"What's up now?"

"The water canisters have got punctured." For the first time there was real anxiety in Arno's voice.

"No water?"

"Not a drop."

"What about the bottles?"

"There's a small amount left in each. Don't you remember me saying we'd need to stop soon and fill them up from the canisters?"

Tom did, but he'd been quarrelling with Josh at the time. He looked down at his brother's pale, sweaty face and suddenly remembered him as a shy child whom he'd once wanted to protect – even though Josh was his big brother. Why had he forgotten that now they were older? Despite the fact that they were opposites, they had got on well together until the last couple of years. Suddenly Josh opened his eyes.

"How do you feel?"

"Terrible." Every time he tried to move Josh winced with pain. "Any water?" Clearly he'd not heard the bad news.

Tom hesitated and Arno came across, kneeling

down by Josh's side.

"We have a water problem," he said gently.

"But there are two canisters."

"Didn't you hear what I said to Tom? They're punctured."

Josh closed his eyes against the grim reality of their plight. "I was asleep," he murmured. He looked as if he'd fall asleep again any moment.

Arno spoke again. "We've got some left in the water bottles, but that's only a little. We need to conserve what we have."

Tom glanced at Arno pleadingly. "Isn't there any water round here at all?"

Arno was studying the map again. "There's a waterhole about three miles away. Could be a little further."

"I thought you knew the area so well." Tom wanted to shift the blame. Wasn't Arno meant to be their guide?

Arno didn't reply and there was a long silence, broken by Josh groaning.

Wanting to walk away from the situation, Tom climbed up to the top of the gully and looked out across the plain, which was vast and featureless. In the darkness nothing was distinct and the grassland looked more like a huge lake, making him even more thirsty. Their predicament was appalling, he thought. However would they survive without water, let alone get back to civilisation and medical help for Josh? Then he realised that being alone with his own thoughts was much worse than being with the others. After all, Arno was in charge. Surely it was his responsibility to get them out of trouble! Of course he'd get them out of trouble. He was a professional guide, hired to show them the sights and look after them if they got into danger. Wasn't he?

Tom scrambled back into the gully, still conscious that he and Josh had always regarded Arno as the ultimate super-guide with everything at his fingertips. But at the moment he seemed to have alarmingly little to contribute.

"I've got a first-aid kit, but it's only designed for minor injuries. Your brother needs to have his leg set. Maybe I can rig up a splint."

Arno was talking as if Josh wasn't there. Who is this

guy anyway? wondered Tom. We don't know anything about him. His fear increased again, turning into a kind of dread at being stranded in this wilderness with a stranger.

"What about that helicopter?" Tom asked tentatively.

"It should come looking eventually, but not for days yet. We've already talked about this."

"*Should?*"

"One of the choppers is being overhauled and that puts a lot of strain on the rescue service. There *is* another aircraft, but it could be out on some other emergency. And with them not expecting us at Kisimu until Wednesday evening…"

"So what are we going to do till then?" Tom questioned aggressively.

"I've got some painkillers and I can give Josh one of those, which will help." There was a brief pause. "We'd be stupid to try and carry him to Matendu between us, even in the morning. Don't forget, this is lion territory. At least I've got a gun, and it's still working – despite the accident. In fact, the gun's about the only thing that *is* working. We have to be careful."

You have to be careful, thought Tom, defensively. It's *your* job to be careful, not ours.

Ska began to bark and Josh's groaning intensified. As a result, Arno seemed even more anxious. He went to fetch the water bottles from the jeep. Three out of the four of them were empty. Arno stared at them thoughtfully, then put them into a shoulder bag.

"Maybe I *should* try and make the waterhole. There's a chance it could be dry, though."

"But you said we shouldn't wander about in lion country," snapped Tom. Make up your mind, he thought savagely. You should be our leader. Not that you're much good at it.

"We don't have much choice, do we? We need water. We're going to have to take a risk."

"Look," said Tom. "Why can't I go for the water?"

"Don't be stupid."

"I'm not." Tom was resentful. "I've done a lot of orienteering at school – as a team sport. I'm good."

"But not good enough for out here."

"What do you mean?"

"This is Africa."

"So?"

"It's the wild."

"Well – are you going to go?"

Arno shook his head. "Not tonight. I should stay with Josh. He needs a splint for that leg and I must put up a tent and rig up a mosquito net for him. Well – for all of us."

"So I'll go for the water."

"Not now. We must wait until morning," said Arno.

"I can't do that." Suddenly Tom realised how incredibly thirsty he was. And there was something else in the back of his mind. He needed to prove himself to Arno after messing up in the jeep. Tom remembered how many times he had done this at school and at home. The climb up the cliff face, the running in the rain, riding a moto-cross bike when he had no experience, the jump across the ditches on the marsh. Why had he done all these things? Maybe to put himself in first place? He didn't know. Maybe to put Josh in *his* place. Second place. But now he had to care for Josh. He had broken his leg and would wake up even more thirsty in the morning. Tom wanted to get water for him, and he wasn't going to listen to their guide – the hired hand. He should be the one to help

Josh, not a stranger, paid for by Dad.

"You'll have to wait," said Arno firmly.

"How would *you* get to that waterhole, anyway?" Tom asked casually.

"I'd use a compass and the map," said Arno, relieved that Tom wasn't challenging him any more. Holding out the map, he showed Tom the compass direction he would follow – north-west all the way.

Arno was in "guide" mode again – relaxed, in charge. Suddenly, acting on impulse, Tom grabbed the map, compass and shoulder bag containing the water bottles from their surprised guide and ran away from the camp, as quickly as ever he'd run in any race.

Arno was furious, shaking his fist and calling out to Tom. "Come back!" he shouted. "Come back *now*."

But Tom ran on, oblivious to his entreaties. He knew Arno wouldn't come after him. He couldn't leave Josh. Soon Arno was only a tiny, indignant figure in the distance.

How on earth would he manage, Tom suddenly wondered, now that he had got his own way. Water? Lions? Living in Ealing hadn't exactly equipped him for survival in a wilderness and he found himself longing for the quiet routine of school and home. But then he recalled how good he was at running and felt an unexpected rush of confidence. Orienteering – finding the route and running through difficult terrain – was his greatest talent, and with his long thin frame Tom was built for long-distance running. Even Josh had to admit that. He'd managed to get away from Arno. But would his running skills help him to the waterhole now?

Suddenly Tom began to panic, sure he'd been a complete fool to run off like this, defying Arno and putting himself at incredible risk. But he *had* to get water. He couldn't possibly last the night without drinking – or so he thought. And he was sure Josh couldn't either. As a result, he'd had to take the law into his own hands. But what had he done?

All too quickly, Tom realised he'd plunged himself into the African bush – a highly dangerous environment which should have been viewed from a vehicle rather than penetrated on foot. Tom paused, listening. It seemed he was surrounded by danger – danger that he had no idea how to cope with.

Thirst

Monday, 8pm

Tom looked out at the darkening plain. It was amazing how safe the jeep had made him feel. Now the vehicle was wrecked, he could no longer be driven through the wilderness. Instead he was on his feet and alone.

Despite the cooling night air, sweat was glistening on Tom's brow as he jogged on. Each bottle would hold about a litre. There was a tiny bit of precious water slopping about in the bottom of each of them. Tom was already incredibly thirsty and felt sure he could drink the lot at one go. Then he realised that if he did find water he could fill a bottle and drink as much as he liked – as long as he put iodine tablets in it first. He could fill all the bottles after that. Cheered by the thought, Tom began to run faster, the ground dry and dusty beneath his feet, the full moon giving the grasslands a strange, silvery sheen.

Fortunately there was still a track, maybe the same one that Arno had been going to follow in the jeep, and this at least was reassuring. Tom glanced back and could just make out Arno and Ska sitting a little distance from the jeep, far away. He didn't think Arno could see him, though. Just as well.

As he ran on, Tom began to realise how out of shape he had become. The three-week holiday that Dad had saved up for for so long hadn't exactly been physically demanding. They had sat on planes and in buses and taxis for what seemed like a very long time, and then, for the last three days, in Arno's jeep. At first Tom had found this frustrating, limiting his appreciation of what they were seeing, but gradually he had grown used to it and to love Kenya. The plain in particular held a magical quality, with stunning beauty and rare animals and a sense of eternity.

Tom kept checking the compass. So far he seemed to be on the right bearing, but he hadn't been running for long and already he was beginning to gasp for breath, his throat as dry as the arid landscape. He was wearing shorts and a T-shirt and a pair of old trainers. They were comfortable, but he wondered if they were going to stand the pressure of the run. A few trees were beginning to appear more frequently now, but they were shrivelled, barely alive, and boulders rose menacingly on either side. He could hear the unfamiliar sound of crickets and they made him feel wary and uneasy.

Tom had always been confident at both schoolwork and sport, and he'd always got on well with his parents. So why did Josh irritate him so much? he wondered. But he knew the answer all too well. For some reason his parents always seemed to cosset Josh, to protect him, while Tom was left to make his own way. Why was Josh such a favourite? He had once asked his father the burning question and had been told, "We don't have a favourite. But Josh finds life a bit more of a struggle, son. Not like you. He needs support." Why should Josh get all the help? Tom had wondered at the time, and still did.

But now their rivalry had plunged them all into disaster and he felt bitterly ashamed of himself for the first time.

Tom was now approaching the foothills and his heart was thumping painfully as he prayed that the waterhole wasn't dry. The promise of water was now becoming an obsession and Tom saw himself lying on his stomach by the side of the waterhole, lapping like a dog.

Again his thoughts turned to Arno. Who *was* Arno? He and Josh were in a serious situation, totally dependent on someone who might turn out to be more unpredictable than they could have anticipated. And here he was, looking for water, leaving his injured brother in the hands of a stranger.

Panic gripped him and Tom had to force himself to calm down. It was natural to him to take the lead – he had no problem with that – and he was reasonably self-reliant. But this unfamiliar, dangerous setting was making him feel distinctly out of his depth. Though Josh was even more so, he thought to himself.

Josh was a couch potato, lying on the sofa, watching as many videos and playing as many games as he could pack into a week. He, Tom, was a highly motivated student, heading for university. Josh was lazy and switched-off, doing as little work as he could get away with, and regularly truanting. While Josh was shy and introverted, practically friendless, Tom was the opposite, with a wide social circle because he had such an outgoing personality.

So was Josh a rebel or just a dropout? Tom didn't know, but what he did know was that Josh hadn't always been like this. At eleven, his brother had been quite fit and athletic, a keen footballer and doing OK at school. So what had gone wrong?

Tom ran on, mouth dry but his speed gradually improving, somehow slipping into the rhythm of his running, drawing on his energy reserves.

Tom checked the compass again and saw that he was still on the right bearing. He must have already covered a couple of kilometres, so where was this water? Tom began to fantasise, seeing a crystal-clear lake with clean, cold water rippled by a darting breeze, but the foothills were as gaunt and arid as the plain, the sandy surface littered with boulders.

In a lapse of concentration, Tom stumbled as the

slope rose again, but as he took up the rhythm of his running he imagined he could at last see water, glinting in the moonlight, beckoning him on.

Tom began to gasp for breath again, his legs feeling like lead, his thirst almost overcoming him as he reached a large dip in the ground and came to a stumbling halt. Clouds were scudding across the moon and he couldn't see anything properly in the relative darkness, but Tom was sure he could hear a soft, lapping sound.

Joyfully he began to move towards the depression in the ground, which was suddenly illuminated by moonlight. But Tom couldn't see any water and his joy turned to despair. This couldn't be the place. The small depression might once have been some kind of shallow dew pond, but now there was nothing but dust.

Could this be the waterhole that Arno had told him to find? Then Tom remembered that Arno had given him no guarantee there would *be* any water.

Tom began to run down towards the hollow, the dryness in his mouth like the dust under his sore feet. Surely there must be something left – even a brackish puddle would be acceptable.

At last he reached the hollow and began to search, but there wasn't the slightest hint of water. Not a drop. Tom could make out some prints in the dust, but had no idea what sort of animal had made them.

Suddenly drained and exhausted, Tom sat down by the dusty bowl and checked his watch. He picked a water bottle and took the last sip of the warm liquid in it. But it was hardly even a single mouthful.

Then Tom staggered to his feet, temper rising, wanting to lash out, to hurt someone in revenge for his bitter disappointment. He picked up some stones and began to throw them at a tree. Then Tom hit out at the air with his fists, and kicked more sand-covered stones around the dust bowl until his blistered feet hurt even more and he began to hop up and down, suddenly conscious that he was behaving like a total idiot. He'd never been violent, although he'd had several skirmishes with Josh, but those had been quickly resolved, either through the intervention of their angry parents or by Josh giving up.

After a few moments of miserable reflection, Tom began to trudge back the way he had come, and then paused to glance down into the hollow, imagining for a wild moment that a secret spring had suddenly filled it with clear water. As he began to jog down the next slope, moving back towards the trees, Tom reversed Arno's directions in his head and turned the compass to match. But although this was simple enough, the moonlight seemed malevolent, changing the shape of the trees and bushes, making him lose his way.

Surely he'd seen those particular trees before? He'd definitely noticed those gnarled and twisted roots, pushing up above ground.

He gazed around at the featureless landscape and the phrase "ill-met by moonlight" filtered into his mind. Wasn't that an extract from a poem he had studied at school? Or a play? Either way, everything certainly looked sinister in the wan light of the moon.

A chomping sound made him jump, and he saw an elephant lumbering slowly away from him in the distance, but then, as he stared past it, he caught sight of glinting eyes in the scrub and Tom came to a stumbling halt.

He stood still, hardly daring to breathe, wondering if the eyes were going to come any closer. A rank smell filled his nostrils and something moved tentatively towards him, but all he could see was a dark shadow. Then the moon lit up the lion cub and Tom started, feeling a short-lived stab of relief. The cub was small, very small. As they looked into each other's eyes, Tom felt protective – as protective as he had once felt towards Josh. Then warning bells began to ring, but for a moment Tom couldn't think why.

Clutching at the water bottles, Tom stood completely still as the realisation flashed through his mind. If there was a lion cub there should be a lioness. Shouldn't there?

The Scent of a Lion

Monday, 9pm

Wave after wave of shock coursed through Tom. He knew he ought to take cover, but he was too terrified to move. And anyway, there was nowhere for him to go.

The smell of lion was menacing, and Tom broke out in a cold sweat, his thirst forgotten. He *had* to find cover. Like now – and fast. Gazing round frantically he saw a tree with some substantial branches, and wondered if he could make it in time.

But hadn't he read somewhere that you had to stand still? Or had Arno told him that at some point during their travels?

Tom couldn't remember.

Then he heard a low snarling sound from the scrub and, with a little gasp of terror, his legs at last began to work. He crept towards the tree and reached for the lower branches, frantically hauling himself further up. Adrenalin surging through him, Arno's bag still intact, in desperation Tom climbed higher and higher until he was able to wedge himself into a fork.

When Tom looked down he could see the lioness below him. Although he was terribly afraid, he didn't think she had seen him. Then suddenly she bounded on, drawing back her lips and roaring fiercely. The sound was primeval, appalling in its ferocity.

Tom climbed even higher again, muscles aching, arms and legs badly scratched. For a moment he hesitated, looking across, seeing the lioness pacing backwards and forwards in a patch of bright moonlight while her cub gazed up at her.

Tom shivered, wondering how long he would have to wait before she went away. He didn't *think* the lioness had seen him – but had she smelt him? He knew, too, that these creatures could climb trees. He wasn't really safe up here. He felt sick as he imagined those terrible teeth tearing him to pieces, providing fresh meat for her and the cub. Tom wondered if lions hunted together. He was suddenly sure they did. Weren't they collectively called a pride – a pride of lions? Might more of them arrive, hungry for his flesh?

Tom knew he had to stay where he was until the lioness was out of sight, but even then she could lie in wait, ready to stalk him.

After some flurried, panicky thought, Tom reckoned he had no choice but to stay in the tree until dawn or even later, until daytime, when hunting animals like lions would be resting. Staring down at his watch in the wan light he saw that the time was just after nine pm. When was dawn? Six am? Seven? The prospect of the night up in a tree seemed endless and of course Josh would be worried out of his mind. And what about Arno? What would Arno do when he didn't return? Even if he had run off without Arno's permission, he was still officially in his care and he didn't want him imagining the worst all night.

But it couldn't be helped. Tom worked himself into another slightly more comfortable cleft in the branches and leant back. After only a few minutes unexpected sleep overwhelmed him. But as he drifted into unconsciousness he began to fall...

As Tom toppled forward, still half asleep, he instinctively locked his legs around a branch and was amazed to find himself swinging upside-down. Terror engulfed him and he reached out frantically for a branch, just managing to right himself again.

Gasping, heart hammering, Tom checked the glade and could see no trace of the lioness. Had she moved away with her cub? Or was she still waiting for him, hidden in the undergrowth. Could there be others, the rest of the pride...

Thoroughly awake now, Tom realised that to try and spend the night in a tree had been a ridiculous idea. Hunger pangs filled him as well as thirst and he felt deeply depressed.

Again Tom looked at his watch. Almost ten pm. Gazing down, Tom still couldn't see any sign of movement or hear any snuffling sounds. Most significant of all, he still couldn't smell the lions' scent any more.

Tom continued to stared down. Was the lioness

anywhere nearby or not? What about the cub? Could they both be lurking in the undergrowth, just waiting for him to climb down so they could pounce?

Tom felt completely indecisive as he tried to work out what was the best thing to do. Half an hour later he was still in the tree reviewing his options. He had never had to make such a life or death decision before, and he was finding it incredibly difficult.

Then Tom froze as he sensed movement. Quite suddenly something striped moved out of the shadows into the milky moonlight and stood there, snuffling the air. As his eyes adjusted to the light, he recognised the creature as a zebra, and when it limped forward Tom guessed it was either old or injured.

The zebra seemed tense and anxious and Tom wondered if it could smell lion, even though he couldn't. Then another zebra arrived, looking much more alert. The newcomer nuzzled its companion, as if to break the spell, to urge it into action.

Tom waited, and so did the zebras. The moon went behind a cloud, but still nothing happened.

After what seemed like ages, the moon came out again and the zebras began to move away from the tree, gradually picking up speed. Then Tom heard a low growl and witnessed the sudden spring of a powerfully muscular body moving at incredible speed. He was reminded of a diving jet fighter plane he had seen on television.

The lioness leapt at the older zebra while its younger companion made a bolt for freedom. Then the jaws of the lioness opened, exposing teeth like tusks. The zebra gave a terrible scream, again and again, as the lioness's teeth bit deep into its throat. Tom closed his eyes, unable to look, but he could hear the crunching of bone. He thought of home, of the hotel, of the safety of the jeep, as he realised yet again, with a chill of horror, that he was at the mercy of the wild. There was a sudden silence, broken only by the sound of the lioness's jaws tearing and chewing.

When Tom finally summoned up the courage to gaze down again, he saw the lioness ripping at the zebra's carcass, helped by her small cub who was tugging rather than tearing, unused to the kill.

After what seemed a very long time the lioness and her cub disappeared into the night, leaving only the head and the now-skeletal carcass of the zebra.

Tom was filled with an all-consuming nausea and panic. He had been gripping the branch so hard that his hands really hurt and when he looked he saw blood on his palms where the bark had cut into his flesh. He couldn't remember ever having been so frightened.

Despite trying to stay awake, Tom drifted off to sleep again. An hour later, exhausted, slowly losing his grip on the branch, Tom actually fell out of the tree and landed with a bump on the ground.

Getting to his feet, carefully checking he hadn't broken any bones, Tom gazed around the darkened glade in creeping terror. Tom was still so afraid that he almost scrambled back up the tree again, but somehow he managed to force himself to stand still. Amongst the trees he could hear the occasional scratching, rustling or tapping sound. Could the lioness still be waiting? Just as she had been for the zebra?

Then, slowly, sweating with anxiety, Tom began to edge forward in the moonlight, sure that he was heading in the right direction, but then losing confidence. He pulled out the compass from the bag, tried to read it, peered anxiously into the undergrowth and then moved more purposefully downhill.

Tom began to run, stumbling occasionally, but somehow keeping to his feet on the uneven ground, gaining confidence, the cool night air making him feel revitalised. But was he being stalked? The rustling and tapping seemed louder, as if there was something large out there in the shadows, instead of dozens of small animals which would do him no harm.

Sweating, gasping, sometimes stopping in his tracks and listening and then trying to run faster, Tom found himself back on the plain where there was no cover at all. Sprinting over open ground, continuously stopping to check the compass, Tom eventually found himself heading towards a pinpoint of wavering light which he soon realised was the glow of a campfire. But he knew sanctuary was still a long way off and, with every step he took, Tom could imagine the lioness pursuing him, those razor-sharp teeth ready to tear him to pieces.

Attack

"How could you run off like that?

Where the hell have you been?" Tom could see that Arno was very angry. But had he been concerned for his safety? Or just about the water bottles?

Unable to tell and feeling both frustrated and guilty, Tom lost his temper. "Where the hell do you *think* I've been?" he bellowed.

"You've been gone for hours. I was really worried about you." Arno glanced at the empty water bottles that Tom had just thrown on the ground. "And where's

45

that water?" He still seemed panicky, which wasn't at all reassuring.

"There isn't any. The hole was dry."

"For God's sake—" Arno's voice was sharp.

"Don't you believe me?" Tom demanded, but when he saw how defeated Arno was now looking his temper drained away. "I'm sorry," he muttered.

"The lack of water's not your fault," said Arno, restraining himself. "But going off to get it without permission *is*."

"Well, there was no chance anyway. The place is a dust bowl," Tom snapped back at him. "And then there were these lions."

"*What?*"

"A lioness and her cub. She didn't see me, I don't think. But I had to get up a tree." Suddenly, Tom needed comfort, but all that was coming across from Arno was intense anxiety. "I had to stay up there and I almost fell out and then she got this zebra and tore the thing to bits and I went to sleep again, and this time I *did* fall out of the tree and started running. I kept thinking she was stalking me. All the way back," he gabbled, ending on a half sob, surprising himself.

Arno held out his arms and without thinking Tom ran into them. Arno hugged him tight and then let him go, giving Tom a slight push and a pat on the shoulder.

"I'm sorry," Tom said again.

"What for?"

"For being a wimp. For failing."

"You didn't fail. You've proved yourself, even if you did disobey me." Arno paused. "Come and sit down by the fire here. I tell you, all the young men at Matendu have to spend a night in the open in lion country. It's a test of courage. A coming of age. Every guy has to take the test and they're all about your age." Arno paused and then continued. "We're out in the wilderness here – but it's not the wilderness you saw from the jeep. This is for real. You can smell and feel the land. You really get to know what it's like – and you get to know yourself much better in the process. Maybe there'd be less trouble in the world if every young guy had to spend a night in lion country."

"In Ealing?"

"Where?"

Tom laughed for the first time, a kind of croaking sound, and some of his tension drained away. "It's on the outskirts of London. Josh and I have lived there all our lives."

"I went to university in London, but I don't remember Ealing."

Tom was amazed, as if Arno had suddenly changed into someone completely different. "You never told us that. What kind of degree did you get?"

"I was studying economics. I got a First."

"But that's – that's incredible."

"What – for someone who's a tour guide?" But Arno was smiling as Tom burst into embarrassed protest, horrified at sounding so patronising. "Yes – I worked hard to get a good degree. I wanted to modernise my father's farm, maybe organise a co-operative. But then the government changed and there was a military junta. I'd been politically active and I had to leave. So I wasted my degree. It'll be a long time before I can go back there – if ever."

"Are you in touch with your parents?" Tom suddenly felt exhausted by their problems and Arno's. All he wanted to do was sleep.

"No. I'm dangerous to them and the telephone is tapped." For a moment Arno looked away. "They know where I am, but it's a lonely business. Look, your brother's asleep. I managed to fix a splint for his leg with a broken branch and I've rigged the tent up for him. I've tried to make him comfy with our sleeping bags too."

"How is he?"

"I gave him painkillers. He should sleep for a while."

Tom was relieved that Arno had looked after Josh well. Now he felt the need to open up. Arno confiding in him had helped. "We've had a bad relationship over the last year," he admitted.

"Why's that?"

"I overshadow him. He thinks I do, anyway. Actually I think my parents go too soft on him—" He broke off.

"That was the problem with my brother, and if I went home the situation would be the same."

"Did he go to university in England too?"

"No. He stayed on the farm and that caused a major rift between us. So you and I have something in common, as well as being stuck here."

"So what are we going to do?" Tom looked at Arno challengingly again. But his suspicions of him had evaporated.

"The first priority is to find water. We can't go on

for long without that."

"Surely they'll be searching for us by now?"

"I told you – we aren't expected at Kisimu until Wednesday. They won't know we're missing yet."

"So we can't count on immediate rescue." Tom was suddenly desperate again. "And the waterhole's dry. This tribe that live at Matendu—"

"They're called the Kala."

"Are we going to try and reach them in the morning?"

"That might not be such a good idea," Arno broke in.

"Why not?" Tom was bewildered.

"I don't usually take any tourists near Matendu. They aren't happy about having outsiders in their village generally – they want to protect their culture. It's very important to them."

"So what *are* we going to do?"

"Maybe if I go to them alone—" Arno hesitated at the look on Tom's face and looked away. Tom's annoyance returned. Why did Arno always try to stop him from doing anything to help?

Then Tom heard the sound of screeching – and jumped up as he realised the screeching was coming nearer. "What's that?"

"Sounds like hyenas. They're Spotted Hyenas round here. They hunt and scavenge in packs." Arno was still sitting down. He didn't seem worried.

"Are they coming to dinner?"

Arno laughed. "I don't think so."

"Suppose the lions come? Don't they hunt in packs too?"

"Lions live in family groups."

The screeching came again, this time even closer. Arno stood up, picked up a couple of flaming branches from the fire and gave one to Tom.

"If they try to get near – throw that in their faces." He sounded casual, as if an attack by wild animals was a routine event.

"Have you been hunted by lions?" demanded Tom.

"Hardly. But I know the main thing is not to run – to face them out."

"Are they likely to attack us humans?"

"Only in defence or if they're very hungry. But there's plenty to eat out here for lions – if not for us. Remember the zebra."

Tom preferred not to remember the zebra at all. He

reckoned the lioness and her cub had been *very* hungry.

Arno flourished his branch and moved a few paces away from the campfire. Ska joined him. Tom followed them, his burning branch held high in the air, lighting up the dark plain.

Then, without a sound, a hyena was there, watching them, lit by the baleful light.

The hyena, looking like a cross between a fox and a dog, was slowly joined by others of varying sizes. They all had dark spots and reddish-brown fur. Although Arno stood his ground, waving his branch, Tom could no longer see any trace of Ska. Without warning, the hyenas turned, making a high, cackling, laughing sound that left Tom feeling deeply afraid. It was as if the hyenas were laughing at them for daring to imagine they could survive in the wild.

"Why are they laughing?" demanded Tom miserably.

"It may sound like laughing," said Arno, "but it's the opposite. They're afraid of us."

As the hyenas raced away into the shadows Tom heard Josh calling out, sounding terrified at waking and finding himself alone.

"It's OK," Tom shouted back. "It's all going to be OK."

"What's going to be OK?" yelled Josh. "What are you doing? Where's the water? What's that horrible cackling sound? Where's Arno? What's going on?"

Josh's stream of frantic questions was drowned by a shrill howling sound that was terrible to hear.

"It's Ska!" shouted Arno. He began to run out into the darkness, and soon the only sign of him was his flaming branch.

Again the cackling could be heard, turning to a roar, and Ska's howls of pain seemed louder.

Tom was horrified. If Arno was killed what were he and Josh going to do? But even at this moment of danger Tom realised how selfish he was being. Ska was enormously important to Arno. He loved him. Without thinking of the consequences, Tom ran out to help Arno, whirling his flaming branch above his head, all too conscious that the flames were only spluttering faintly above him.

Then Tom saw Ska loping towards them. The dog seemed to be covered in dark blood from head to tail, and in the dying light of the flames Tom could see a long gash down his flank. But now where was Arno?

Tom began to shout, to bellow out his name, while Josh was still plaintively calling out from the tent. The hyenas were still screaming, sounding as if they were encircling their camp.

Then, to Tom's great relief, he saw Arno running towards him, his eyes fixed on Ska. The screeching and roaring of the pack of hyenas came again, but now they seemed to be moving further away.

Ska ran for the safety of the campfire and then collapsed, whimpering. Arno knelt down beside him, tearing off his T-shirt and attempting to staunch the blood that was gushing from the wound in his side.

"Get me a towel!" he yelled at Tom. "They're in the back of the jeep."

Tom ran towards the vehicle, running round Josh in the tent.

"What's been happening?" Josh asked weakly. "What's that awful noise?"

"Ska's been attacked by something," Tom gasped as he searched for the towel. "Try and keep calm. We've got to stop the blood."

"Where's the lion?"

"It wasn't a lion. Lions don't screech."

"Are you sure?"

"Don't be so pathetic. They were hyenas," snarled Tom as he raced back to Arno, who grabbed the towel out of his hand, tore it into strips and began to wrap them tightly round the dog's body. Ska was whimpering now and giving little grunts of pain as the strips of towel pressed against his wound. "How much blood has he lost?" asked Tom.

"Not too much. I just have to stop the flow."

"Why were those hyenas so aggressive?" asked Tom. "I thought they were going to attack us. And look what they've done to Ska."

"We're on their territory – and they don't like that."

"But people drive through all the time!"

"The animals accept jeeps and trucks in the day. But at night it's hunting time. And they don't accept humans getting out of their jeeps and trucks. We're well and truly out of ours."

As he spoke, Arno continued to press down with the pieces of towel while Ska, lying on his side, gazed up at him.

"I think I've staunched the blood," Arno said at last. "Get me the first-aid box. This is going to be tricky."

"What's happening?" asked Josh yet again as Tom rummaged around in the wreck of the jeep, finding the first-aid box at last.

"We're dealing with Ska's wound."

Josh tried to sit up and then winced. "Is he going to be OK?"

"Think so. Are you in pain?"

"I'm desperate for some more water. Arno said you ran off to find some. Where is it?"

"I didn't find any." Tom suddenly felt inadequate – not a feeling he liked.

"You idiot!" rasped the enraged Josh. "I suppose you were looking in the wrong place."

"I was looking in the *right* place." Tom was defensive. "The exact spot Arno showed me on the map. But the waterhole had dried up. Anyhow, I've got to get back to Ska."

Josh grunted something and Tom could see that his brother was as self-centred as ever. And as much of a waste of space.

Arno soaked some sterilised wadding with disinfectant and carefully packed Ska's wound with it. At first the dog yelped and struggled, but Tom held him firmly while Arno wound a thick bandage round his middle and tied it tightly. Then he secured the bandaging with a safety-pin and elastoplast.

"He may scratch the whole thing off," said Arno anxiously. "And if he does the wound will get infected." He stroked Ska's head and he grunted a little and then closed his eyes. "He'll sleep now anyway." Arno paused. "How's Josh?"

"Desperate for water."

"Well, unfortunately I've given him both the mangoes we had and all the water we can spare. A couple more painkillers will help him," replied Arno. "Then I'll build up the fire and we'll all get some sleep. We can't do anything without that first."

Tom wondered if there was anything they could do anyway. Weren't the odds totally against them? No one knew yet that they were stranded. The helicopter rescue service might be too busy to search for them anyway. The animals didn't like them on their territory and some of them could already be closing in. They had little food and water, and no plans to get any. On top of all that, their only potential rescuers were the Kala who Arno was so much against anyone disturbing but him. But surely Arno wouldn't leave them here alone?

Arno was still crouching down by Ska. But he suddenly glanced up at Tom, as if aware of his anxiety. "Look – I'm going to get you both back to safety," he said. "It may take a bit of time, that's all."

Kitu

As Tom dragged himself into his

sleeping bag he felt something move between his toes. Something that was dry and rubbery. He gave a terrified yell and pulled himself out of the sleeping bag as fast as he could.

"What's happening?" asked Josh.

"Something wrong?" Arno sounded exhausted.

But Tom was already shaking his bag out on to the ground and in the wan moonlight he saw something slithering over the ground. "Snake!" he shouted. "I've probably been bitten! What the hell am I going to do?"

Tom began to panic, breaking into a cold sweat, sure the snake bite would be lethal. Maybe he only had minutes – seconds – to live.

But Arno had also caught sight of the snake and began to laugh.

"What's so funny?" bawled Tom.

"What's going *on*?" said Josh.

"I've been bitten by a snake. I'm going to die! So what's so funny, Arno?"

"You're not going to die," said Arno, still laughing.

"Why not?"

"Because that's an African House snake – and it's completely harmless."

"You're sure about that?"

"Absolutely sure."

"Tom!" called Josh. "What's all that about dying?"

"Nothing," replied Arno. "The snake's harmless. Now let's get some sleep."

Feeling a complete idiot, but deeply relieved at the same time, Tom snuggled back into his sleeping bag.

Tom slept fitfully, squashed between Josh and Arno, grateful for their body heat for the remainder of the cool night. He was continuously woken, sometimes disturbed by Josh's groaning, but most of the time because he wasn't sure he trusted Arno to take them to the Kala. The worry kept niggling away at him.

Completely exhausted, Tom wondered if his fatigue was making him unnecessarily suspicious. Surely Arno wouldn't desert them, would he?

After an hour or more of wakefulness, Tom at last fell into a light sleep, dreaming about running in the foothills through the sparse sanctuary of the trees until he reached the dried-up waterhole. But in his dream the hole was filled with ash that drifted slowly up into the sky, stirred by a gentle breeze.

Tom woke to a blinding headache and a rough tongue licking at his face. It was Ska. He had survived the night and hadn't tried to tear off his bandage. The dog was weak and limp, but at least he was still alive.

Tom sat up and Ska transferred his licking to Arno who showed no sign of waking.

Josh had stopped groaning and was snoring loudly.

Tom got stiffly to his feet. The early morning was bright and sunny and he could already feel the heat building up. So was his thirst, forgotten for a while but now back with a vengeance, his throat so dry that he wondered if he was going to be able to speak.

Last night Arno had divided up the food supplies and carefully rationed the remaining bottle of water. They had each sipped at the warm water in the bottle, but there was hardly any left. It had only made Tom feel more thirsty. Glancing down at his watch, he saw the time was just after seven.

Tom gazed out at the plain, and although it was still a little misty, this couldn't disguise its size. He felt completely dwarfed by the sheer scale of the view and had the unsettling feeling that humans were nothing, mere specks in a primeval world that had existed for thousands of years before they came – and would exist for thousands of years after they were dead.

The plain was the lions' territory – not theirs – and their survival couldn't be guaranteed for even the next few hours.

Then Tom saw a cluster of stunted trees a few metres away and, even better, a bush on which there was a gleam of dark fruit.

How could they have overlooked it? He began to run

towards the trees, oblivious of danger, and finally ended up in their inadequate shade. Sure enough the bush had clusters of dark red berries, succulent looking, almost certainly full of juice that would go at least some way to slaking his thirst.

He had to try one, but suppose they were poisonous? Deciding to ignore the possibility, Tom still remembered to gaze round, sniffing the air for the scent of danger, realising as he did so that he was quickly adapting to life in the wild. Then he shoved a berry into his mouth, biting eagerly, but quickly choking in disgust. There was no juice and the fruit had an unpleasant taste that reminded him of soap.

Bitterly disappointed, Tom spat it out, watching it fall to the ground. When he looked up he was amazed. A boy was running through the trees.

Tom could hardly believe his own eyes. The boy was short and sturdy, wearing shorts and running barefoot. Could he be some kind of mirage? A trick of the light?

"Hey there!" Tom bellowed, and the stranger hesitated, took a nervous look at him and then quickened his pace. "Stop! You've got to stop!" Tom began to panic. The boy would know where food and water were. If he let him go, Tom would be stuck with the dry berries that seemed to mock him. "Stop!" Tom yelled again. "You've *got* to stop!"

But the boy simply increased his speed again and Tom burst into a run. Despite his exhausted and dehydrated condition, he *had* to catch up with him.

"Please stop!" yelled Tom again. "*Please* stop," he pleaded, but the boy just increased his speed. Tom did the same, knowing the boy was essential to his survival – to the survival of them all. Soon Tom was running faster, with the kind of effortless ease he relied on when he needed to win.

Now he was actually within metres of the boy, who made the fatal mistake of slowing slightly to look back. Without thinking about consequences, acting entirely by instinct, Tom threw himself at the boy's legs, rugby-tackling him to the ground.

They began to fight, punching and kicking as they rolled about, but Tom soon realised that although the boy was about his own age he was much stronger than him. Within a very short time the boy was kneeling on Tom's shoulders, pinning him down.

"Stop!" shouted Tom. "You've got to help us!"

The boy began to talk fast in a language that Tom couldn't understand. Then he got up and prepared to move away again, kicking Tom in the side with his bare foot, a kick that really hurt. But Tom staggered to his feet and tackled him again. He was fighting for his life; for water and food – for survival. Somehow his desperation drove him much harder and now it was his turn to pin the boy to the ground.

"You've got to help us," gasped Tom over and over again. "You've *got* to help us. You've – got – to – understand – you've – got – to – help – us."

Then there was a bark and Tom turned to see Arno running towards them, with Ska limping behind.

The boy began to struggle again, but Tom still had him pinned down when Arno and Ska arrived.

"What the hell are you doing?" Arno demanded.

"He wouldn't stop."

"Let him up."

"No way. He'll know where the water is," gasped Tom. "Water and food."

The boy began to speak that strange language again

and, to his relief, Tom realised that Arno seemed to understand him.

"He'll help us. Let him up!" Arno grabbed at Tom's shoulder and pulled him off the boy.

"I didn't mean to hurt him. What's he saying?" asked Tom.

"He's saying you attacked him," said Arno furiously.

"He wouldn't stop."

"His name is Kitu. I'm going to ask him if he'll help us to find water – and food." Arno and the boy started to speak in a strange musical language, full of sibilant sounds. They seemed to be in agreement with each other.

A wave of glorious relief filled Tom. He'd been right all along. He'd had to stop the boy – Kitu. Suddenly there was hope again. "Where does Kitu come from?" Tom gasped.

"He's one of the Kala."

Kitu stared at Tom curiously and Tom stared back at him. Kitu looked as if he might be his own age. Like Tom, he was thin and wiry. He looked confident and relaxed – very unlike the way Tom was feeling. He turned to Arno and asked him abruptly, "How do you know the Kala's language?"

"They speak a kind of Swahili, as do most Kenyan tribes. I've learnt Swahili since being in Kenya, and it's taught in all the schools too. Why do you ask? Don't you trust me?"

"Yes," Tom stammered, caught off-guard. "At least—"

Arno grinned, but he seemed too preoccupied to notice Tom's slip. "We're in luck. Kitu has told me how to get to Matendu. I'll set out later on. He will try and help me to persuade them to assist us."

"Why not now? We need—"

"Because he's on a run – a kind of training run – and he's going in the opposite direction."

"So what?" Tom was getting angry again. "This is an emergency. What about Josh? And Ska?"

"Look," Arno rapped out. "These people don't need us. We need them. So if we want help – which we certainly do – we have to co-operate with them. But fortunately for us Kitu is going to run past a waterhole which he says is full. Get all the bottles, put them in the bag and go with him. You'll be safe with him. I need to look after Josh. He was feverish in the night."

"Will Kitu wait for me?" asked Tom.

"You'll have to keep up with him," said Arno. "And you'll have to come back here on your own. I'm not really comfortable letting you do that. But I suppose we don't have much choice..."

"Can't you insist he comes back with me?"

"I can't ask him that," Arno said quietly. "You'll have to try and keep up with him. Kitu's doing an important test. Part of the test is that he has to get to his destination and back to Matendu quickly and we've already held him up a bit. We have to respect what he's doing. He's training for his initiation rites. I've already told you that this is very important to members of the Kala."

"I'll try to keep up, but Kitu mustn't lose me! I don't know what we'll do if we don't get water soon." The very thought of water made Tom's thirst unbearable.

"He knows that," replied Arno. "He'll try not to lose you."

But Tom didn't feel so sure about that.

"Look, if you want to keep up with him you need to do two things. Remember to breathe through your nose – and keep your mouth closed. That way you won't lose so much saliva—"

"And the second thing?" asked Tom.

"Get some breakfast down you and put on loads of sun block. I'll ask Kitu to wait."

Kitu set a gruelling pace from the very beginning as they both began to run, Tom a few paces behind him.

Kitu's running seemed effortless, and although Tom kept up for a while, he soon began to waver. Despite all his competitive running back in England, Tom knew he was no match for Kitu – and he hated it.

After a while the clumps of twisted, dried-out trees with their scanty shade began to thin out and they were out on the dusty plain with no protection from the sun. Tom was wearing a baseball cap and dark glasses, he had loads of factor-50 sun cream on, but still his arms and legs felt as if they were burning. Soon his whole body was soaked with sweat, his feet were sore and his shorts had chafed his thighs badly. Nevertheless, he carried on for kilometre after weary kilometre, just about keeping Kitu in reach, but knowing he couldn't keep up the pace indefinitely. Dust clouds were blowing up on the horizon and his throat was now so dry that any attempt at swallowing was painful.

The mysterious acrid dust clouds reached them all too soon and even Kitu was coughing, head-down, trying to push himself on. Then Tom heard a distant, rumbling sound that he couldn't identify. Was it thunder? Heavy rain? His head buzzed with alternatives, all becoming increasingly bizarre.

The immense thundering sound was coming from the dust cloud which was growing thicker by the minute, and suddenly Kitu turned and came running back towards him, flinging himself down in a shallow hollow in the ground and trying to dig himself into it. In a split second, Tom realised that the dust cloud was not some kind of natural phenomena, but a cloud made by animals moving very fast. Soon he could dimly make out a herd of buffalo thundering towards them.

In a flash Tom joined Kitu face-down in the hollow, and tried to dig himself into it as well. But the ground was baked hard by the sun and he realised it would be impossible to do so in time. The buffalo were fanning out all over the plain, perhaps only fifty metres away from them now, their hooves making a relentless drumming sound that was coming nearer and nearer.

Tom glanced across at Kitu and saw that he'd actually managed to dig his way into the hard soil a little more. His hands and feet must be exceptionally strong, Tom thought, desperately scrabbling again. But it was already too late.

Tom closed his eyes and kept them closed, expecting any moment to feel the crushing weight of the herd on his shoulders. For a few ghastly seconds, he visualised a scene from a cartoon, with his body flattened to a plank and being pushed under a door. He almost laughed aloud at the horror of the idea. Then he was surrounded by the buffalo, their massive hooves pounding as the herd thundered round him. So far he hadn't been crushed, but how long would his luck hold? Tom wondered, his throat even more caked, the blinding sun and the noise of the charging herd completely overwhelming.

For the first time in years, Tom began to pray, pressing himself desperately into the hot earth as the herd thundered past him.

Suddenly, something warm and wet hit his back.

He soon realised that he had just been covered in slimy manure.

Then, all at once, the stampede was over and the deadly drumming sound was fading into the distance. Tom looked up for a moment, his eyes stinging, to see the dust cloud slowly clearing. But before he could even register relief at having miraculously survived, he felt another stab of terror. To the far right of him and Kitu, hazy and undefined in the distance, was a lioness.

Tom realised that there were three of them. But the lionesses seemed to have no interest in him and Kitu. Straight away they were off, pursuing the herd of buffalo with a deadly, focused purpose.

Tom had never felt so weak and distraught. He got to his knees and remained head-down, unable to struggle to his feet. The sun, a ball of fire in a steely blue sky, made the midday heat unbearable, and sweat was pouring off him, dripping into the grey sand. He began to cough. Dust had got into his throat and nostrils; it was also making his eyes itch badly.

After a while Tom was conscious of a strange sound. Then he realised he was listening to human laughter and saw Kitu staring down at him, laughing wildly and pointing at the buffalo dung that was spread all over his shoulders.

Tom didn't appreciate the joke. He stood up, glaring at Kitu, who now seemed to want to make amends, sprinkling his shoulders with handfuls of sand and dust to prevent the smell of dung attracting clouds of flies. Then Kitu began to laugh again. Suddenly, to his immense surprise, Tom heard himself joining in.

He and Kitu made eye contact for the first time and Tom saw – or thought he saw – a look of liking, even respect, in Kitu's eyes.

Tom immediately felt much warmer towards him. Kitu was on warrior training and he, Tom, was just about keeping pace with him. He felt a rush of pride.

Then Tom saw that Kitu was looking at him with a different, strange expression on his face. He felt he must have been far too optimistic. What's Kitu trying to tell me with that look? wondered Tom. That he's going to leave me here? Why *should* he wait for me after all? Kitu's training run is at stake. Why should he forfeit that for a stranger?

Whatever it was, Kitu was obviously determined Tom should understand it. Now he was crouching down beside him, drawing something in the sand. What on earth was it? All Tom could see was a mass of meaningless,squiggly lines. Then Kitu got to his feet, threw out his arms and ducked his head. He looked as if he was diving. Why should he be diving? Suddenly Tom's hopes rose. You dive into water, he told himself. That's it – you dive into water!

Tom looked down again at the squiggly lines in the sand and thought he could make out a circle round them. Was that meant to be a lake? But what did the other lines mean? He shrugged his shoulders and Kitu looked impatient; he began to use his fingers, holding them up one by one.

"Time," croaked Tom aloud. "Are you telling me how long to get to a lake, or something?" But Tom knew as he spoke that Kitu wouldn't understand a single word he was saying.

They both shrugged, but then Kitu's face lit up. He grabbed at Tom's watch and stared down at the sand-covered dial, wiping at the surface with his forefinger, nodding and holding up four fingers on his right hand. Then he closed his palm and began to raise one finger at a time.

"Four hours?" asked Tom hopelessly.

Kitu held up his fingers, one by one, all over again and nodded, smiling at him. But Tom felt deeply depressed. Four hours to the waterhole. He'd never be able to walk for four hours, let alone run.

But Kitu was already starting off, without looking back at him, and somehow Tom forced himself to follow. Now the plain was slowly, almost imperceptibly, sloping down and he felt he had a bit more energy.

Soon Kitu stopped and beckoned Tom to join him. The slope was steeper here and Tom was looking down at something unbelievable. Kitu must have meant four minutes rather than four hours! Below them, in a shallow valley, surrounded by more stunted trees, was a hole. A waterhole which actually contained a brown-looking, muddy liquid. They'd arrived. Ecstasy filled Tom and he gave vent to a whoop of glorious joy.

Within a couple of minutes Tom was in the water, splashing about, the wonderful wetness soaking into his clothes, his skin. The dung and dust soaked away. He had never felt such extreme happiness before.

Tom wanted to stay in the muddy waterhole for

ever, but he was still really thirsty. Then he suddenly remembered Josh, Arno, and Ska and felt ashamed. Dragging himself out, he filled the three water bottles and put iodine tablets in them. They looked alarmingly small, but he knew they would have to do. Tom glanced at his watch. It was just after twelve. He knew he had to wait an hour or so until the iodine tablets dissolved and purified the water.

Tom had been told that when he got to drink the water it would taste odd because of the iodine, but he wasn't worried about that. Anything wet would be wonderful.

Kitu was watching the whole process with interest but he said nothing. Tom wondered how much further Kitu had to run to complete his day's training before he would turn round and go back to Matendu. Why shouldn't Kitu take him with him all the way and then back again to the jeep? Suddenly Tom remembered the radio. Why hadn't Arno asked Kitu about that, back at the jeep? Tom knew *he* would have no chance of making Kitu understand if he tried to find out if the Kala had a radio himself.

Now Tom was feeling cooler and a little rested, he

realised how strong his hunger pangs were. Breakfast had been hours ago and he'd had no supper the night before. Suddenly, he had the idea of getting supplies from Kitu's village.

"How far to Matendu?" he asked Kitu, holding up his fingers hopefully, but Kitu only grinned at him.

Tom saw the grin as a taunting sneer, the smile of someone who was playing with him. Again and again, getting more and more irritated, Tom mimed eating. It was so important that Kitu should understand him! But again and again, he only smiled in response. Then, without warning, Kitu turned away, beginning to run.

"I want food," yelled Tom, racing along beside him. "You have to take me to food!" He then ran across Kitu's path and stopped him in his tracks, grabbing him by the shoulders and shaking him. "Food!" he screamed, completely losing his temper. "You've got to help me find food!"

Kitu's face was expressionless. But he swiftly drew back his fist and hit Tom as hard as he could in the stomach.

*

When Tom's breath came back, Kitu was a speck on the far horizon. He was alone. He still had the three filled water bottles, but would he be able to find his way back to the jeep? Josh and Arno would die of thirst unless he did.

He got shakily to his feet and picked up the bottles and put them in Arno's bag. Then Tom gritted his teeth to begin the long, hot, dangerous trek back to Arno and Josh.

After he'd been jogging for an hour or so in the midday heat, Tom was finally able to drink from one of the water bottles. He wanted to gulp down pints, but he intended to save as much as possible for Josh, Arno and Ska. After a few sips he screwed the cap back on firmly. Running over the hot and dusty plain was a terrible test of endurance, but he was determined to succeed. At least he hadn't seen any dangerous animals this time, and wasn't very likely to. It was daytime – they should be sleeping now.

By the time he was into the second hour of the return journey, Tom was so exhausted he was beginning to hallucinate, and several times he staggered and fell.

He kept picturing his life in England – the crowded streets and the fast food chains, imagining he was walking into his favourite pizza restaurant, sitting down and consuming a large slice of pizza and then another and another, washed down with ice-cold Coke and then an equally ice-cold milkshake.

Staggering on, the plain endless around him, the food fantasy seemed just as painful as the thirst he had endured earlier. Each step was becoming an enormous effort; his legs felt leaden and sometimes buckled under him.

Then, in a moment of reality, Tom saw in front of him a scattered tree-line and knew he was at last approaching the wrecked jeep. There was the sound of barking and he saw Ska loping stiffly towards him, the bandage still intact around his middle.

Tom suppressed a sob and then let go, almost sobbing his way back to the gully he now regarded as some sort of home. Ska limped up to him and Tom knelt down and threw his arms round the dog's neck.

Brothers Alone

Tuesday, 4pm

Exhausted, Tom lay on his back, looking up at the hard bright afternoon sun and having his face licked vigorously by Ska. Then he felt strong arms lift him up to a sitting position and water being poured down his throat.

He slowly came to, not sure where he was or the identity of the man who was pouring the water into his mouth. Tom spluttered and struggled, now recognising Arno and managing to push the bottle and its precious liquid away. "Slow up," he rasped. "That water's over two hours away. We've got to ration it."

"It's OK," said Arno with a confidence Tom couldn't understand. He passed Tom some bread.

"Have you had some water?"

"I will."

"Aren't you thirsty, for God's sake?"

Arno put Tom's bottle down, picked up his own, gently grabbed Ska and poured water down his throat. It was only when Ska seemed satisfied that he took a short drink himself.

"You trying to prove something?" asked Tom aggressively.

"No," said Arno. "Are *you*?"

They were silent.

Then Arno said, "You did well."

"What about the food?" demanded Tom even more aggressively. "It must have almost run out. Why didn't you tell Kitu that he should take me to the end of his run, then on to Matendu. Instead of *you* going I could have done it."

"Water was our top priority. Matendu's a really long way you know – and I was worried enough as it was about having to let you go for the water and come back alone. You wouldn't have been able to keep up with Kitu all the way," said Arno with brutal honesty. "You did really well to make it to the waterhole with him and then get back by yourself."

"But what are we going to do when our food runs out?" demanded Tom.

"I'm going to reach the Kala later tonight. If they have a radio I'll use it. And hopefully, by tomorrow morning we'll be back with a stretcher. I'll bring back some rations."

"How did you work that out? Are you telepathic or something?" Tom asked sharply.

"I spoke to Kitu about that. There was no way I could interfere with his run. So I—"

"Why didn't you tell me?"

"There wasn't time. Look—" Arno paused. "We're in a tough position. You've done so well. You have to learn to trust me. I'm trying to make the best decision for us all. But Josh has complications."

Tom looked up at the sun and shivered despite the boiling afternoon heat. "What do you mean?" he asked quickly.

"He was running a fever last night."

Tom was worried. "Did anyone come to look for

us?" he asked, though he knew it was a forlorn hope.

"There's been no sign of a helicopter or a spotter plane."

"So why don't you go for help right away?"

"I'm going soon. Directly I'm satisfied that I can leave Josh."

"What can you do for him anyway?" Tom heard himself ask. But he was scared. What if Josh was dying?

"I've got the first-aid kit," replied Arno, sounding defensive for the first time. "And there are still some painkillers left." He paused and looked at Tom appraisingly. "Why are you always so aggressive? Why *can't* you trust me? I've been on a couple of first-aid courses out here. I *do* know what I'm doing."

"I'm sorry," muttered Tom. "Ever since we had the accident I've been so, so terrified I don't know what to think."

Arno suddenly relaxed and grinned at him. "You're doing really well."

"Have you ever had an accident before?"

"No. I'm always very careful."

He paused and once again Tom felt ashamed. It

wasn't Arno's fault that they were in this predicament. It was his and Josh's.

"I've got to be satisfied that your brother's going to be OK before I set out," said Arno. "It's not ideal trying to make it by night but we don't have any choice now. I'll leave Ska and the gun with you – not that he's up to much with that wound. I've built up the fire, and you'll have to light it directly the sun goes down. You're unlikely to be attacked with that burning fiercely, but you'll have to be careful. I need to rely on you to keep the fire going. As I said before, if I can make Matendu by about midnight tonight I can bring back a stretcher party by late morning."

Tom struggled to his feet. "I can handle it," he said firmly, pushing the thought of another night, alone in the wild, to the back of his mind.

"Thank you," said Arno. "Now, let's talk the situation over with Josh. But first of all let me get you a sandwich."

"Is that my ration?"

"Double rations." Arno went to the jeep and pulled out a box. He opened it and gave Tom a curled-up sandwich. Tom devoured it. He had never eaten anything that had tasted so good.

"You haven't told Josh you're planning to go to the Kala?"

"He wasn't in any condition to be told anything earlier. And I had to wait for you to get back." Arno paused and looked at Tom. "Don't forget – once the sun goes down you can't afford to let that fire go out, however tired you are."

"What did you say about trust?"

Arno grinned and for the second time Tom felt a real warmth between them.

Tom staggered, his legs suddenly feeling weak after his long run, and Arno put an arm round his waist. Tom slung the bag of water bottles over his shoulder as they walked slowly towards the jeep while Ska loped behind them, still limping.

Tom was shocked by Josh's haggard appearance. He was sitting up under his blankets, back propped up with sleeping bags, his face white, strained, and pale in the shadows made by the tent.

"How are you feeling?" asked Tom brusquely. He was often bad-tempered when he was afraid.

"My leg hurts."

"Try some of this," said Arno, handing Josh the water bottle.

They both watched his eyes open wide with delight and disbelief.

"Thanks." Josh drank the water blissfully, holding the bottle carefully with both hands.

After a while Arno said gently, "That's enough. You're going to have to ration the water for a while at least."

"How much have we got?" Josh was instantly anxious again.

"Only what's left of a bottle each. But don't worry. Now let me tell you what I'm going to do."

Arno began to explain to Josh what he was going to attempt that night and to show them both how to fire the gun.

"You should have gone earlier," said Josh irritably. "Why wait until now? Why didn't you get that kid Kitu to do it for you?"

Tom winced. Josh sounded so selfish. But then hadn't he been the same way? He'd assumed that Kitu – and the Kala – should drop everything to meet *their* needs. For the first time Tom realised that Arno was right. He was just as demanding as Josh, and aggressive with it. He felt ashamed.

Arno replied to Josh with a weary patience. "I couldn't leave you, Josh. You might have got a lot worse. I did tell Kitu what had happened to us, but I need to speak to the Kala personally. They're going to need some convincing that I should bring you into their lives in the first place. I *think* they'll help us – but I can't be absolutely certain. I will do my very best to persuade them. At least I can speak some of their language. Tom's in charge of the fire, but he might have to go and get more fuel." Arno glanced round at the sparse trees. "As you can see there's not a lot of spare wood around, so I suggest that Tom makes it a priority to try and build up a further supply, in case you both need it. Take Ska with you, Tom. He'll sense if there are any lions about and give you warning." Arno took a couple of swigs and then gave his water bottle to Tom. "Take this. You've got three half filled bottles – three half empty bottles if you're a pessimist – so be sure to ration them." Arno got to his feet and stroked Ska's head. The dog began to whine as if he already sensed that Arno was going to leave them.

"My leg's killing me," said Josh faintly. "I don't think I can take the pain much longer. Just when are you going to get me to safety?"

"Arno will be back as quickly as he can," said Tom, with a confidence he wasn't quite feeling.

Then he saw Ska looking up at Arno, completely dependent on him, and he felt a rush of reassurance. Arno would never walk out on his beloved dog. Tom *had* to put his trust in him fully, even if he hated being dependent on anyone other than himself.

"We'll ration the water carefully," he said. "And I'll start getting more firewood in."

Arno waved once and didn't look back as Ska began to howl. But once he couldn't see his master any more, he lay down resignedly by the ashes of the fire. Tom thought about their parents. They wouldn't even know that he and Josh were lost in the Kenyan grasslands right now. Tom wished he could see his mum and dad. They would be so worried about their sons when they didn't arrive at the hotel in Kisimu. Then Josh spoke, interrupting Tom's anxious thoughts.

"It's getting dark," his brother complained. "You'd

better go out there and collect some wood. We need to have more in case we run out. Leave Ska and the gun with me."

"No chance." Tom was indignant. "I need some protection too."

"What about me? I'm helpless. I'm a sitting duck!"

Tom felt the familiar anger with his brother building up again, but he tried to hold it back. "OK," he said reluctantly.

Suddenly Josh repented. "You'll be vulnerable out there. Take the gun and the dog with you."

"I think *you* should have them," said Tom, and then realised he was competing with his brother again – this time as to who could be the most self-sacrificing.

"For God's sake!" Josh yelled. "Go and find some wood. It'll be too dark for you to get a stockpile together if you don't hurry up!"

But Tom still hesitated. Josh was right in a way – he *was* completely vulnerable to attack. At least he had a chance of getting up a tree. Why hadn't Arno thought of that? But would Ska even stay with Josh? And what use would an already injured dog and a gun be to a badly injured boy, in the event of an attack by lions?

"I'll get going," said Tom, and patted Ska on the head. "You stay with Josh, Ska. Stay."

But Ska got up and began to limp after him.

"I shan't be long," he said.

"Long enough for me to be eaten alive," muttered Josh, true to form.

Ska sat down and watched Tom begin to collect wood. There was more than he had expected, and he gathered as large a pile as he could carry and walked back to base and then went out to collect more, still followed by Ska. Josh seemed to have fallen asleep – so Tom felt less concerned about him.

By the third journey, Tom was exhausted again, but he still wasn't sure if he had enough wood to keep the fire going all night and he daren't give up.

Josh, now awake again, nagged at him. "That's not nearly enough," he kept saying.

At first, Tom ignored him and just went off again, still faithfully followed by Ska, but when Josh made the same complaint on his return Tom lost his temper. "Why don't you shut up?"

"I'm only advising you."

"Advising me? How could a fat slob like you advise anyone?"

Josh switched to pathos. "I'm in pain – all the time."

"You *are* a pain," Tom shouted as the light suddenly faded. "All the time. Wherever you are." He suddenly wanted to hurt his brother as much as he could. "It was your fault we crashed in the first place."

"How do you make that out?" sneered Josh. "You think you're always in the right, don't you? That's how you con Mum and Dad. Every time."

Tom was silent, surprised by the intensity of his brother's bitterness.

"You've always got to get in with people, haven't you – like you tried to get in with Arno."

"I don't know what you're talking about."

"Yes, you do. You've always wanted to score off me. You've got to be the best and the fittest, haven't you? You skinny idiot!"

"Yeah, well, the reason you're fat is you don't take enough exercise. And you eat junk food all the time."

"If I didn't have this broken leg, I'd kill you!" Josh replied.

*

Tom took some time inexpertly lighting the fire Arno had laid. But eventually the wood spluttered into flames.

"OK," said Tom. "Let's have a sandwich. Maybe it's hunger that's making us so bad-tempered." He went to the box, pulled out a sandwich and split it in two as evenly as he could. But even then Josh complained he'd got the smaller piece.

All at once Ska began to howl and sat shivering, looking up at them both as they argued. His howling continued until Tom went over to him and began to stroke his head. "All right, Ska – it's all OK. Everything's OK."

"That's just what it isn't." Josh's voice shook. "I'm so worried – and think of how Mum and Dad will feel!"

"I know. I'm sorry." Tom suddenly wanted to make amends. They couldn't go on like this – not if they wanted to survive. "And you're right. I know I try to be the best at everything, but I didn't realise it got to you so much. I can't help it – I'm just competitive, I suppose. I'm sorry."

"It's too late for that now. You've no idea what it's like to be sidelined all the time." Josh sounded desolate and for the first time Tom realised what damage their constant rivalry over the last two years had done to his brother.

"I'm going to get some more wood," he said hurriedly. "The fire's going out and we need more wood ready to add to it."

Josh didn't reply and Tom began to walk back towards the trees.

Suddenly he heard Josh's voice, half a sob and half a sneer. "It's already out. Why don't you build it up again now?"

Silently Tom fetched matches from the jeep.

"How many have we got left?" asked Josh.

"Half a box at least – and there's another full one. We're OK."

"Don't waste any of them. We're not OK. We could be here for weeks." Josh took a slug of water.

"Watch that," said Tom.

"You watch those matches!" snarled Josh.

"OK." Tom squatted down, determined not to give in and have another slanging match. As he added and lit more of the dry tinder with a shaking hand, Ska licked him. Tom found the lick particularly comforting. At least Ska liked him. He had been shocked to realise how much Josh had come to hate him – and that it might have been partly his fault.

Tom watched the comforting blaze of the fire from the trees as he and Ska returned for the fifth and, hopefully, last journey. Then Ska stiffened. Tom gazed at him, wondering what he could hear. There was no smell of lion, so maybe something else had disturbed the dog. But what? Then Tom could hear Ska growling, and feel his hackles rising. Were they being stalked again?

Tom listened, standing stock-still. Perhaps he should get back to the safety of the campfire, but he remained where he was, listening, sniffing the air while Ska continued to growl.

There was a hoarse cry from Josh. "Tom!"

"What is it?"

"There's something moving."

"Shut up!" hissed Tom.

"What?"

"I said – shut up!" yelled Tom, throwing away caution. Why was Josh such an idiot?

But there was danger.

"There's something moving," said Josh again.

"Stay still."

"I can't do anything else," Josh's voice broke. "You know I can't."

Tom said nothing and then began to walk quietly out of the trees, his heart thumping painfully, dripping with sweat. He continued to head back towards the fire, followed slowly and reluctantly by Ska. Could there be a lion out there? Or were their imaginations so sharpened that they were frightening themselves for nothing?

Tom hoped to God they were.

Night Fright

Tuesday night

Suddenly the smell of lion was overpowering. But Ska was no longer growling. He was silent and shivering, looking up at Tom as if trusting him to solve everything.

"Tom—" began Josh.

"Shut up. Where is it?"

"What?" Josh's voice was quieter.

"The lion."

"I could only hear something moving," said Josh, shrill with fear now. He was holding the gun, but he was shaking so much Tom doubted he could do much good with it.

Tom swore to himself and gazed round at the overturned jeep and Josh's inadequate tent.

Where was the thing waiting? Waiting to pounce... With sudden decision, Tom grabbed a burning branch from the fire and held it high above his head.

As he whirled the branch around, the flames sparked and spluttered, partly lighting up the gully, and Tom thought he saw a shadow, waiting patiently on the other side of the jeep, silently watching them. Determined to stand his ground, Tom shouted and waved the burning stick.

But the shadow didn't move.

"Go away!" The instruction sounded pathetic – probably to the lion as well, thought Tom miserably.

His mouth was now so dry he couldn't get any more words out, inadequate or otherwise.

The shadow padded nearer, but it was still impossible to make out what it was.

"Get out of it!" Tom suddenly found his voice which was sharp with fear. He knew he couldn't cope much longer. He'd done as he'd been told and stood his ground, but the trick didn't work. Arno had been wrong. Horribly wrong. Then he saw the eyes, staring out of the darkness at him. They looked oddly curious. Then the creature came nearer and Tom saw to his horror that the shadow had become a lioness.

She moved steadily nearer and Tom could see the sheer force in her muscular body, poised to spring, poised to devour him. He could imagine those teeth slashing at his flesh, grinding their way through to the bone, and he remembered the fate of the zebra.

"For God's sake—" shrilled Josh. "Do something – or it'll come and get us both!"

The lioness was still staring at Tom.

"Do something," quavered Josh.

"Why don't you shut your mouth?" Tom lost all control, bellowing at the top of his voice, and at the intensity of his rage the lioness unexpectedly began to back off. Now beside himself, Tom ran towards her, screaming out in anger and frustration, whirling the still flaming branch around his head. Amazingly, the lioness continued to back away.

Then, taking an enormous risk, Tom flung the flaming branch as hard as he could in her direction. It fell metres short, but she turned and began to pad away.

As the lioness disappeared amongst the trees, Tom began to sob, trembling all over, in such shock that he could hardly believe he had actually defeated the enemy.

Eventually Tom came over to Josh's shelter, crawling in beside him.

"You saw him off," whispered Josh. "You actually saw him off."

Tom gazed at him in silence. Then he said, "He was a she."

"I was terrified. And I've never heard you in such a state. You seemed to lose all control."

"I was so afraid – sure I'd fail." For the first time in a long while Tom needed Josh's reassurance.

"Anyway, you amazed me." There was genuine regard in Josh's voice.

"I amazed myself." Tom laughed and suddenly relaxed, gazing up at Josh lying in his tent with genuine affection. "Are you OK?"

"Sort of."

"How much pain are you in?"

"I was so scared I forgot it for a bit. But the pain's

there all right – it's a kind of constant throbbing."

"What are we going to do?" Tom suddenly felt helpless again. Ska nudged at him gently, needing human company.

"You're asking *me*?" Josh was surprised.

"Yes."

"We've got no choice. We'll have to wait for Arno."

"Do you trust him?"

"Yes."

"Why?"

"I think he's a good person. He left us the gun. And Ska."

"Is that all?"

"Isn't that enough?" asked Josh. "You know, he could easily have taken Ska with him. And the gun."

"I guess so," said Tom doubtfully. Then he added hastily, "That's what I thought."

"So we're thinking alike. For the first time in ages."

Tom started. Josh sounded amazingly mature. Why hadn't they ever talked like this before? Was it because he had always wanted to have the upper hand – that he had always *needed* to have the upper hand?

"I'm sorry."

"What about?" asked Josh.

"I haven't – we don't exactly get on well. We haven't for a long time."

"It's my fault too. I gave up."

"Gave up what?" asked Tom.

"I can't compete with you, Tom."

"Who asked you to compete?"

There was a long silence. Tom knew the answer. *He* had.

"Do you think we'll get out of this mess?" Tom spoke again, eventually.

"If we trust Arno."

"So he'll be here in the morning?" Tom still needed reassurance.

"I'm sure he will." Josh's tone was almost fatherly.

"And if he isn't—"

"He'll be here."

The brothers were silent for another moment.

Then Tom said, "I'll go and tend the fire."

"Do we need any more wood?"

"Let me take a look."

Tom got up and walked over to the still blazing fire.

Then he came back to Josh. "I think we've got enough. Why don't you try to get some sleep?"

"What are you going to do?"

"Keep watch," said Tom.

"Can't we both do that? If you'll help me, I can get into a better position to see what's happening."

Tom hesitated. "But you need all the rest you can get."

"Don't you?"

Suddenly the thought of sleep was of paramount importance to Tom. But again he hesitated. "You're in pain."

"Maybe that's an advantage." Josh gave a hollow laugh. "I can't sleep properly anyway."

"OK." Tom was no longer hesitant. "We'll take shifts. What can you see from there?"

"Not enough."

"Where do you want to be?"

"Nearer the fire."

Tom entered the tent, removed the blankets and put his brother's arm over his shoulder and tried to pull him up to a standing position. But Josh began to yell.

"This *is* going to hurt," Tom told him. "Try and

hop on your good leg."

Josh was moaning in pain now. Tom looked down at his dead-white face. Sweat was standing out on his brother's forehead.

Eventually they managed to cover the few metres between the upturned jeep and the fire. Josh was incredibly heavy, but after what seemed a very long time Tom managed to lower him down by the fire. He fetched the blanket to help make him comfortable, and slowly Josh's whimpering subsided.

"We made it," said Tom, gasping for breath.

"Sorry I made so much noise."

"Sorry I hurt you."

"You couldn't help that."

Tom realised that they had never talked like this over the last couple of years of rivalry.

"Let's have half a sandwich," he said.

"Some celebration," muttered Josh. But he looked pleased.

"I can't see Ska." Suddenly Tom realised that the dog wasn't there. He went back to the wrecked jeep and began to call out his name, but there was no sign of him. Tom picked up some more blankets and Josh's water bottle – which was almost empty.

"He's just wandered off." Josh didn't seem worried.

"That's just what he shouldn't be doing. We haven't even got a torch." He pulled a blazing stick from the fire and held it up above his head. "I'll have to find him – for Arno's sake."

"Don't leave me alone!"

"I'll have to." Tom felt a pang of regret, sensing their new-found relationship was already under pressure.

But Josh rallied. "Sorry. I'm just being selfish. You *do* have to find Ska."

"I can't think where he's gone." Tom called his name over and over again, but there was no reaction. The darkness of the night seemed leaden and heavy. "I'll go and take a look."

"OK."

"Shan't be long."

"Maybe Ska's gone off to find Arno?"

"No way – he'd have done that before," said Tom reassuringly.

He strode away, the burning branch above his head, calling Ska's name continuously. Then he heard something. Could the sound have been an answering bark? He plodded on. Tom reached the stunted trees and then he saw the dog crouched over something on the ground.

He gasped as in the light of his flaming branch he saw the half-eaten body of an antelope. Ska was tearing at the thing, devouring the soft, raw flesh. He was obviously desperately hungry. For a moment, Tom wondered if he should somehow hack out a lump of meat and roast it over the fire for them all. Theirs had been a very frugal supper and he still felt ravenously hungry too. But he couldn't let the dog eat raw antelope, could he?

Tom grabbed at Ska's collar and tried to pull him away, but the dog's jaws were firmly clamped on the antelope's flesh. The dog obviously hadn't satisfied his appetite yet and he growled as Tom yanked at him again, using all his strength.

Ska refused to budge, growling fiercely now, determined to continue his feasting. But Tom was relentless and eventually succeeded in dragging him off.

Then Ska pulled back hard and Tom was forced to let go of his collar once more, the branch with its guttering flame still gripped in his other hand. As Ska limped back to the carcass, Tom followed him, trying to pull him away again. In the struggle he dropped the branch. The dying flames lit up a small part of the surrounding area, illuminating for a terrible moment a pair of shining eyes.

Tom gave a cry of terror and began to run, while Ska raced ahead, running hard despite his wound towards the safety of the fire.

"What's happened?" Josh cried out.

"Ska was gorging himself on a kill. Then, then—" Tom was gasping for breath.

"Then what?" Josh interrupted him.

"A lioness," said Tom, beginning to gabble. "I'm sure I could see her eyes staring at me. Quickly, where's the gun?"

Josh began to whimper with fright as he scrabbled about in his blankets, reaching for the weapon. But suddenly a zebra broke cover and ran past their fire at high speed.

"Correction!" Tom shouted. He felt completely light-headed with relief. "Not a lioness – a zebra!"

Matendu

Josh and Tom spent an uneasy night.

Tom had intended to keep awake during Josh's watch but in the end, however hard he tried, he couldn't stop himself nodding off to sleep, waking with a jerk to an early dawn that was cold and bleak with an overcast sky. The great plain stretched mistily around them, and Tom shuddered at its enormity. The vast expanse made him feel small. He wasn't worthy of rescue. What had he achieved in his life? Nothing but a state of enmity with Josh that had landed them all in their present predicament.

Josh, meanwhile, was staring ahead, watching the flames of the dying fire, and Tom staggered stiffly to his feet. He piled on more wood and then, shivering, came back to sit down with Josh.

"Why didn't you wake me?"

"I would have if there was any danger."

"That's not the point."

"You needed to sleep. You're the able-bodied one." Josh yawned. "I tried to ration the water." He held up his bottle which had hardly been touched. Tom was impressed.

"You should still have woken me."

"Do shut up," said Josh, but there was no anger in his tone. "God – I'm hungry."

"So am I."

"We've only got a very small amount of food left. Well, almost none. Just an apple each," said Josh.

"How about roasted antelope?" Some of Tom's initiative returned.

"*What?*"

"A young antelope. The lion's half-eaten kill that Ska found. I was thinking of bringing some back to cook last night, before I got sidetracked!"

Josh swore. "I'd eat anything."

"I'll go and check it out."

"What about the lions?"

"To hell with the lions. They can't do all the eating round here," Tom joked, but Josh didn't laugh. Checking his watch Tom saw it was just after six-thirty. He shivered. "It's cold."

As he turned and began to clamber out of the gully on to the endless plain, Ska loped after him, whining a little, and Tom knew his wound was hurting. He checked the bandage and wondered if he should try to put on another. Then he decided to wait for Arno to help him with that when he came back. Sniffing the air, Tom waited tensely before approaching the antelope carcass, but there was no smell of lion and Ska loped along beside him, seemingly confident.

When they arrived, the carcass had been reduced to skeletal remains. Flies were already buzzing around what little meat was left. Big birds were hovering above. Tom thought at least two of them were vultures. Then a maggot crawled out of one of the antelope's eyes. Suddenly Tom wasn't hungry any longer. He looked at Ska, and noticed that he made no attempt to go near the carcass either.

"Come on, boy." Tom began to run back towards the gully and Ska followed.

"We'd get food poisoning if we ate any of that carcass," said Tom, "even if we cooked it. The meat's crawling with maggots."

Josh looked disappointed, but still seemed to want to be companionable. "OK. Let's hope Arno'll be on his way soon."

Tom sat down by the fire and disconsolately stirred at the dying embers with a stick. The clouds were clearing and he could see the bright orb of the relentless sun slowly appearing. Soon they wouldn't need the fire. Soon, he prayed, Arno will come.

As Tom began to nod off, he could hear Josh beginning to snore lightly. Sleep could be a fatal mistake, he thought, but once again there was nothing he could do to keep himself awake.

As Tom woke again he was sure he was still dreaming, because he was looking up at Arno's face. He was grinning. Tom closed his eyes, knowing his imagination was mocking him. Then he opened them again.

Arno was standing beside him with Kitu and two other boys. They had brought bread, beans and rice.

"You came back," muttered Tom as Arno stroked Ska's head. "I can't believe you're here!" He felt a wonderful surge of joy that he wanted to share with Josh. He turned to see that his brother was fast asleep. For him, the miracle was still to occur. First picking up a piece of bread, then stuffing it with beans and rice, Tom gently shook his brother awake. Josh's eyes opened slowly and unwillingly. Then came a look of total bewilderment.

"Hungry?" asked Tom.

Josh grabbed at the food and began to shove it into his mouth with his bare hands. There was blissful contentment on his face.

Arno gave Tom some more of the bean mixture, wrapped in another piece of flatbread, and Tom began to eat voraciously, mumbling replies to Arno's questions.

"You seem to have coped with surviving the night pretty well," said Arno eventually. "We've brought a stretcher for Josh and we should get going as soon as we can. Do you have any water left?"

Josh picked up his water bottle and so did Tom. "And there's yours," he said, indicating the still half-full bottle lying by the fire.

"You did a good job on the rationing too," observed Arno, still stroking Ska.

Kitu and his companions were gazing at Tom and Josh with interest. They were barefoot, but all three were dressed in shorts and T-shirts. Tom eyed Kitu warily, but there didn't seem to be any animosity in Kitu's stance in spite of their previous encounter.

"The Kala aren't in some stone-age time warp, you know," said Arno, seeing Tom's look of surprise at the well-made light wooden stretcher the boys had brought with them. "They just choose to keep out of civilisation's way, that's all."

"Good for them," said Josh. "I never did like civilisation – not our over-competitive kind, anyway." He and Tom were both eating ravenously.

"Eat more slowly," said Arno. "You don't want to throw it all up!"

But all Tom could think of was the wonderful taste of the beans, mixed with the filling bread and rice. He knew Josh felt the same. They were both oblivious to the future, living only in the deeply satisfying present.

After a contented silence, Arno spoke again.

"This is Kitu, and two of his friends – Lana and Tasin."

"Good to meet you," replied Josh, still unable to take in what was happening. All three Kala boys smiled at him, seemingly able to understand that he meant to be friendly even if the words were foreign.

Then Arno sat down beside Tom while the three Kala boys took a rest. They lay on their backs around the remains of the campfire and drifted off to sleep.

"Aren't you ever tired?" asked Tom. "Even Kitu and his mates are knackered."

"I *am* tired," said Arno. "But I have responsibilities to your parents. I've got to turn this situation round and I'm nowhere near doing that yet. And Josh needs urgent medical attention." He paused and then said, "Do you trust me now?"

Tom nodded, still eating, reluctant to admit his earlier lack of complete faith in Arno.

"You didn't trust me until I got back, right?"

Tom nodded again.

"I do understand," said Arno. "But now I've proved myself, we've got to be able to work together more closely."

"OK," said Tom slowly. "And I've had an idea. If the camcorder's still working we could make a video about what happened and where we're going and leave it in the jeep. That way, if anyone finds the wreck, they'll discover the camcorder, and play the video. Then they'll find out where we've gone."

"That's great, Tom!" said Arno. "I'm with you all the way." He went to find the video recorder in the jeep.

"It's working!" said Arno eventually. "The camcorder's working. Who's going to do the talking?" he asked.

"You're the guide," said Josh. "You do it."

"Can you work one of these?" Arno turned to Tom.

"You bet I can."

"OK. Let's go for it."

Tom took hold of the camcorder and lined up the shot, checking the built-in microphone was also undamaged.

"Ready," he said at last.

Arno stiffened and began to speak self-consciously.

"My name is Arno. I have been taking Tom and Josh Trent on a camping trip. We were due back at the Grasslands Hotel in Kisimu on Wednesday night. But there's been an accident," he said. "Tom and I are OK, but Josh has a broken leg. We've sought the aid of some members of the Kala tribe who are going to stretcher Josh to Matendu. Matendu is approximately thirty kilometres north-east of this spot. Please make your way there with an ambulance. Obviously Tom and I are staying with Josh at all times."

Tom switched off the camera. "Where shall we leave it?" he asked.

"In the jeep itself. The rescue services will find the video. You can be sure of that." Arno sounded confident, but Tom wasn't so sure now.

Neither was Josh. "When *are* they going to start searching for us?" he asked.

"My company and the hotel manager at the Grasslands Hotel both know that we're due there at six tonight. If we haven't returned by then, they'll start looking almost straight away."

Tom was worrying about something else. "Are we going to be able to keep up with the Kala boys?" he asked Arno, anxious as ever about his fitness.

"They'll wait for us if necessary. They've agreed to help us now. Besides, they'll be carrying the stretcher, they won't be moving as fast as usual"

"And the lions?"

"We'll take that risk."

"Do the Kala really have a special relationship with the lions?" asked Josh, obviously hoping that might provide the whole party with protection.

"They're not lion tamers or anything," said Arno. "They have a healthy respect for them and try to keep out of their way! But some of their customs still have their roots in their mythology about lions."

"What customs?" asked Tom curiously.

"Well, it's part of the initiation rite to run through lion country. Like Kitu. And they admire the lions' courage and strength – lions are symbolically important to them and they have lots of legends about them." Arno got up and Tom sensed the subject was closed, though he was keen to hear more.

Half an hour later, Josh was lying on the stretcher that was to be carried by the boys. The heat was much fiercer than yesterday.

"We have to start moving," said Arno, rubbing Ska's neck.

Tom noticed that he hadn't changed the dog's bandage. "I was going to try and dress that wound again," said Tom. "But I thought I might just make a mess of it."

"I'm not going to touch him now. I want to put on a proper sterile bandage when we get to the settlement." Arno paused. "And thanks for looking after him," he added.

From the very beginning of the journey, the Kala boys took it in turns to run with the stretcher as if portly Josh was no weight at all. For once, Tom felt proud of his brother. He was in great pain as he was levered on to the stretcher, but he'd tried hard to resist crying out.

Lana and Tasin went ahead, carrying Josh. Then Tom slipped into a jog with Arno, leaving Kitu and Ska to bring up the rear. But even with his wound, Ska seemed to be able to bound along steadily, and Kitu was enjoying his company.

"You must be proud of Josh," said Arno. "And I'm

proud of Ska. They're both putting in a huge effort."

"How long have we got to go?" asked Tom.

"We'll be there by late afternoon."

Gradually the terrain began to change as the stretcher-bearers left the plain, and reached undulating hills that eventually led to another higher plain that was just as stark and dusty. A track had been beaten across its centre. Here Lana changed over with Kitu who started sharing the carrying of Josh on the stretcher with Tasin.

Tom felt a sudden desire to share the load, despite the fact that he was already exhausted.

"Won't they let me help to carry Josh?" he asked Arno.

"No."

"Why not?"

"They wouldn't let me carry him, let alone you. I'm not nearly fit enough."

"I could have a go," began Tom.

"Why do you need to prove yourself to them?"

"Because I feel like a useless wimp," muttered Tom.

"And what about me?"

"You don't care."

"So why do *you* have to prove yourself, Tom?" Arno sounded a bit irritable. "Don't you think that's rather immature?"

Tom considered that. Then he said, "This initiation test. Is it really important to them?"

"Yes. Once they've completed the tests, they've proved themselves to be men, and they don't need to carry on doing so all the time."

Tom thought what a relief that would be.

Almost as if he was reading Tom's thoughts, Arno went on, "They're not complicated like we are. And we're complicated because we live in so-called civilisation. Here it's tough – but more straightforward."

Tom was very interested, but also secretly wondering how much longer he could go on. Despite the heat Arno and the stretcher party seemed completely resilient, easily able to keep up a steady jog.

Half an hour later, however, Kitu shouted out and he and his friends set the stretcher down gently in the shade of some flame trees.

"There's a waterhole," said Arno. "Just down that track. We're going to stop so Lana, Tasin and Kitu can get a drink and we can have a short rest and fill our water bottles."

This particular hole was fed by a spring and was much fresher and larger than the last, so Tom knew he didn't have to put iodine in the water. Tom filled up the bottles. He and Arno went to sit down with Josh, still on his stretcher, who eagerly grabbed the precious water and began to drink.

"How do the Kala live?" asked Tom.

"They're small-scale farmers, with animals and crops. The terrain is dry and dusty, but there's just about enough water for them to cope."

"Do they get visitors?" asked Josh curiously. "Like tourists?"

"No – they don't allow them in," replied Arno. "We're an exception. The Kala know they live in a fragile world. We need to help preserve it as well."

"How do you feel?" asked Tom, turning to his brother. "You're not sunburnt?"

"No. You put plenty of factor-50 on me, and the other bits of me are covered up. Lana and Tasin and Kitu carried me really gently too," said Josh. "It was like I was floating."

"Go and get some more water, Tom," said Arno, getting up. "Fill the bottles right up and then we must get going again."

Grabbing the bottles, Tom asked Josh quietly, "How are you *really* feeling?"

"Lousy."

"In pain?"

"Yes. It's not sunburn though. There's something else."

"What?"

"I'm still so thirsty, yet I've just drunk a whole litre of water."

"I'll fill this lot right up," said Tom, not liking to tell Josh that he thought he might be feverish again. Or could he have sunstroke? Tom thought not – they'd been careful to cover him up against the sun.

Josh's voice penetrated Tom's thoughts harshly. "Don't be long. How far have we got to go?"

"I don't know."

"Are we about halfway?" asked Josh, his face full of pain.

"Maybe," said Tom. What else could he say?

*

Tom ran down to the waterhole and the small natural spring that bubbled so miraculously from the earth. The three boys were lying on their stomachs, drinking again.

Then Kitu looked up, got to his knees and beckoned Tom over, making room for him. A surge of pleasure filled Tom. He was accepted.

Tom lay down and began to drink. The spring water was soft and cool and a far cry from the much muddier, iodised water of yesterday.

Tom filled the three bottles once again and was about to take them back when Tasin grabbed his wrist. "Mpira?" he asked and pointed at Tom. "Mpira?"

Tin hadn't a clue what he was talking about.

Then Kitu mimed kicking a football.

"Mpira," Tasin repeated.

"Football?" asked Tom. "You're talking about football?"

This time Tom mimed kicking a football and Lana, Tasin and Kitu nodded enthusiastically.

Tom grinned at them and they grinned back. He realised they had something in common.

*

When Tom got back to Arno he said proudly, "Mpira."

"How did you pick that up?" asked Arno. "That's Swahili for football."

"Tasin told me – or at least they mimed and I guessed."

Suddenly Josh gave a cry of pain.

Arno and Tom went over to the stretcher and gazed down at him. His face was covered in sweat. In fact his whole body was covered in sweat.

Tom forgot all about his breakthrough with the Kala boys. Suppose Josh died? Suppose there was no chance for him? He had a terrible mental picture of breaking the news to their parents. *"I'm afraid Josh didn't make it."* Tom shook his head as if to remove the terrible vision of his parents' grief.

"He'll be OK," said Arno as Lana, Tasin and Kitu came back from the waterhole. "Don't worry."

But Tom wasn't convinced.

The Kala

Wednesday, 6pm

Now that he had eaten and drunk his fill, Tom jogged beside the stretcher, closely followed by Arno and Ska. He was relieved to find he was feeling fit and well now, as if he could jog for miles, and when he glanced at the Kala he could see that they, too, weren't showing any signs of strain.

As he ran, Tom's mind ranged over the experiences of the last few days and he wondered where it was all leading them. He felt increasingly anxious, knowing that anything could happen out here on the plain.

Africa was going to test him, like a Kala boy, and he wasn't sure if he could pass.

Slowly, as the afternoon went on, the terrain began to change, the plain giving way to more foothills that were much drier and dustier than before.

"We're not far from Matendu now," said Arno.

"What kind of welcome are we going to get?" asked Tom.

Arno didn't reply.

They arrived at dusk.

After hours and hours of seeing no one, of almost floating through the landscape, it was hard to believe the settlement was real. There were a number of huts which seemed to be made of dried-mud bricks, about a dozen of them, closely circling a larger round building.

"The Kala must be a very small tribe," said Tom.

Arno laughed. "They live in family groups in different locations round here. I think there are about five hundred of them in all."

"Did the Kala make a collective decision not to go into the big towns?"

"Yes, I suppose it could have been a collective

decision. But these people have always worked with cattle. Nothing much has changed – except they've adopted clothes that are sold to them by traders."

"How do they pay the traders?" asked Tom.

"They make money by selling herbal remedies. The Kala use the remedies themselves and trade what they don't need with a supplier."

Kitu and the other boys gently carried Josh into one of the huts and for a moment, Tom felt uneasy, wondering if he would ever see his brother better again. Now the Kala boys had gone, Tom felt a sudden longing for the authorities to step in and sort everything out.

"The radio!" he gasped. How dould he have forgotten? "*Do* they have a radio?" he asked Arno urgently. "Can we contact the rescue services – our parents?"

"No."

"Why didn't you tell me?" Despite his exhaustion, Tom was furious. "You can't mend a broken leg with herbs."

"You'll be surprised what they can do," Arno gently explained. "And they'll make him a much better new

splint. Josh will soon be well on his way to recovery."
But Arno sounded anxious too.

"What about the fever?" Tom was getting increasingly worked up.

"They can bring his fever down."

"How?"

"With herbs. But I can see I'm not impressing you."

"You're not. Why couldn't we have made for an air strip or a town?" Tom said, thinking of ambulances, white-tiled hospitals and modern drugs, all of which seemed a world away.

"Because all those amenities are a long way off. We had to get help for Josh as quickly as possible and I knew the Kala would be able to provide some," said Arno defensively.

"Do you normally take your clients to the Kala for medical help?" Tom realised how absurdly pompous he must sound. But the more he looked around him, the more alienated he felt. He longed for the safe and noisy streets of Ealing. He was thoroughly unsettled by the Kala: their village seemed so primitive, their world so different from his own. He felt as frightened of them as he was of the lions.

"No," replied Arno calmly. "But I know other guides who have. Stop being so negative."

"It's hard," said Tom. "I'm sorry." He meant it now.

They walked over to the hut where the boys had taken Josh and found him in semi-darkness lying on a straw mat. He still looked very ill.

"Any pain?" Tom asked.

But Josh didn't immediately reply. Tom could see his brother's body was still soaked in sweat.

"I'm really worried about him," he hissed at Arno, but Josh heard him.

"I'm not in pain any longer." His voice was muffled and distant. "What's happening to me? It's like I'm drifting." There was a pause, and then he asked, "Am I dying, Tom?"

"No. The Kala are helping you." Tom forced himself to sound confident.

"What kind of help?"

"Their herbal medicine."

"You're going to be all right." Arno was trying to reassure Josh now, and Tom was grateful.

"Why am I drifting?"

"You've got a fever, but you'll feel better soon."

Tom knew they were going round in circles and felt a stab of devastating homesickness for his parents. Mum and Dad would have sorted all this out in no time, he thought – although Tom had no idea what they could actually have done.

"What's that building?" Tom asked Arno warily when they left the hut to make way for some members of the Kala to minister to Josh.

"The big one? It's where everyone eats. Do you want something?"

Tom suddenly realised that despite all his worries he was also incredibly hungry and thirsty again.

Arno led him into the dark interior. The Kala were sitting in family groups, eating what seemed to be some kind of vegetable stew.

Tom was conscious of being watched with curiosity but not with hostility. The old people wore robes made of some kind of roughly woven fabric. The very young children were completely naked, but everyone else wore shorts or skirts and T-shirts.

Arno went to the pot and ladled some of the food into two wooden bowls. On the other side of the room were gourds of water and cups that looked as if they were made of clay.

"Help yourself," he said.

They took their cups and bowls back to a clear part of the room and sat down together on the floor. There must have been about forty of the Kala and they ate in silence, listening to a woman whose voice rose and fell in an almost musical pattern. The huge space was lit by candles which flickered and glowed.

"She's one of the storytellers," whispered Arno.

"What's the story about?"

"It's about how a member of the Kala rescued a wounded lion cub, and received its heart. It's just a myth, of course," Arno added hurriedly.

Tom was enjoying his portion of vegetable stew. Washed down with water that was cool and fresh, the stew was simply delicious. As he ate and drank, the exhaustion seemed to ease and Tom felt increasingly alert, his head clear and concentration focused. But all he could think about was Josh, and the more he thought about him the more concerned he became. He was sure his brother was seriously ill. Would the Kala really be able to help him?

The storyteller's rhythmic voice eased some of his tension, but it couldn't take his mind off Josh. To Tom's surprise he suddenly became aware of an overpowering feeling that, in spite of all their differences, he loved his brother. That must be a first, thought Tom.

At last, when the meal came to an end, they went to check on Josh, only to find him sleeping peacefully, a gourd full of a brown liquid by his side.

"The herbal remedy?" asked Tom, sniffing at the gourd suspiciously. But the smell was soothing, almost like mint tea.

"At least the stuff seems to have sent him to sleep," said Arno. "But the fever hasn't broken yet."

Josh's skin was hot and his breathing was shallow.

"Can they really help him?" asked Tom, beginning to panic again. "Isn't there any way we could get him air-lifted from here?"

"I'm going to talk to one of the elders. He's the most friendly to the outside world. His name is Laris."

"Was he at supper?"

"No. He's on his way back from one of the other settlements."

"Have you met him before?"

"Only once. On a trek."

"So he doesn't go into any towns either," said Tom in disappointment.

"Yes he does: he's the one who takes the herbal remedies to their supplier, and sometimes brings back western-style clothes. He speaks English – he's the only member of the tribe who does. He learnt the language from some missionaries when he was a child." As Arno spoke, an elderly man with grizzled grey hair and a beard came into the hut. He was slightly built, but had an air of authority that was immediately noticeable. "This is Laris," said Arno.

Laris didn't attempt to greet them, but looked down at Josh in concern.

"Your brother's very ill," he said quietly.

"Can't you do more for him?" Tom was now sure his worst fears were justified.

"We are trying. Come and talk outside."

Tom followed him out of the hut, feeling quite frantic with anxiety. He was now even more certain his brother was going to die and there seemed to be nothing anyone could do.

*

The night was cold with a chill wind. The main building was in darkness now and so were the surrounding huts. A small fire spluttered on the edge of the settlement and Laris went to sit in front of it. As Arno and Tom joined him, Tom decided he must speak to Laris more strongly. He realised he had been counting on the Kala to have a radio or a miracle cure and now even that hope had gone.

"I've got to get my brother to a hospital," he said.

"That won't be possible at the moment," replied Laris gravely. His expression and the tone of his voice never seemed to change. It seemed as if he had a total, deeply frustrating acceptance of fate.

"How far is the nearest town?"

"The air strip is about twenty-five miles away. Your brother cannot make a trip like that. Not at the moment."

"So how can you help him?"

"We have remedies for fever. I'm confident he'll come through."

"What about his broken leg?"

"That's easier. We can splint his leg again in a less improvised manner. We're doing that right away."

"Isn't there some way we could get Josh to this air strip?" Tom felt a burst of uncontrollable panic.

"I'm not sure he would survive the journey."

"He survived the stretcher journey here!" Tom caught a warning glance from Arno. "I'm sorry. I don't mean to be rude, but my parents don't know where we are and they must be frantic with worry."

Laris nodded. "I understand. I wish we could help you get to them. But that's impossible."

"So you really don't have a radio?" asked Tom desperately.

"We have nothing like that. We've never wanted too much contact with the outside world. It would undermine everything we believe in – everything that we are." Laris paused. "But you are welcome to stay with us until your brother is better and more able to stand the journey."

There was a long silence. Then Tom said, "We've got no choice. But my parents will think we're dead. Unless the rescue services find the jeep and check out the camcorder video no one will know we're here."

Laris sighed and then said, "There is another possibility."

"What's that?" asked Tom.

"If you are really fit, like a Kala boy, you could run to Triano. It's the air strip at Osak. From there they would be able to send a helicopter back here to pick up your brother. But the journey would be very difficult, perhaps impossible. What do you think, Arno?"

"It's grasslands for most of the way, filled with lots of predators. Lions, for instance," added Arno ominously. "I don't fancy anyone's chances over such a long distance. I mean, you've got fit young boys here, trying to become warriors, but a trip to Osak would be even further than the longest distances they run. And they know the terrain." He paused. "But then so do I. So I should be the one to go."

Laris shook his head. "It's too near the Ugandan border. If you were arrested your family would be at risk. But you're right. It would be too much for Tom."

Tom looked at Arno and Laris. He seemed to make his mind up. Then he asked, "What kind of terrain is it?"

"Much the same as this. Hills and valleys at first in this highland area, and then of course the plain. It would be very dangerous."

"Even so," said Tom with a sudden fierce determination, "I want to have a go. I'll get fit by training with Kitu, if he'll let me."

There was a fraught silence and then Arno said, "I should go myself. But Laris is right. Osak *is* on the border with Uganda." He looked worried. "I could be arrested – but I'll still try. You should stay here with Josh. I'm responsible. I'm your guide."

"No," said Tom. "You can't put your family in danger. You can run with me part of the way, but then I must go on alone." He paused, surprised at his own sudden resolution. To anyone in England the idea would seem suicidal, but Tom clung to the fact that when he was running with Kitu, being paced by Kitu, he had gained so much confidence that he had run faster than he had ever run in his life. Then he said, "There is one thing. What about Josh?"

"You don't know if you can trust us to look after him?"

Tom felt acutely embarrassed and tried to smooth over the situation. "I'm sure you'll take good care of him."

"Please trust us," Laris said. "I would be grateful for

that." He paused and then added, "You are welcome to run with Kitu tomorrow, but you must not interrupt his warrior training any further. His final run is not towards Osak, but to Burundi. And I must insist you don't hold him up tomorrow."

"So you will let me train with Kitu. You think I could make it—"

Laris gave Tom an enigmatic glance. Then he got up and walked out of the hut.

There was a moment's silence. "Now I've blown it," said Tom. "I'm sorry, I didn't mean to annoy him by going on."

"You haven't. I've got a lot of respect for you, Tom, and I want to give you some advice."

"What's that?"

"Don't attempt Osak."

"Why not? I'm a good runner." Tom was immediately indignant.

"I know, but you'd need a lion heart for *that* run."

"No," said Tom as if he was talking to someone who was much younger. "You just need extraordinary stamina. With some training I can build up more stamina."

"Josh needs help very soon. There's no time for you to train properly. It's better for me to go."

"*I'm* going," said Tom. "It's down to me – whatever you say."

"And you'll leave your brother here?"

"I reckon it would be better if you stayed with Josh. You speak the language – you can look out for him properly."

"No way," said Arno sharply. "I owe it to your parents not to let you do this."

Tom paused. Then he replied, "But you owe it to *your* family not to endanger them by going all the way to Osak, Arno!"

Arno stared at Tom in silence. "Let's leave the decision to Kitu," he said at last. "Run with him tomorrow and if he reckons you can keep up then I'll take you part of the way – but after that you'd be on your own." Arno looked searchingly at Tom. "You'll still need a lion heart, you know."

Tom went outside on his own to think. The situation was very serious and that shouldn't be side-stepped. But he thought it wasn't only the Kala boys who had to successfully pass their initiation rites. He, Tom, had to do the same. Josh's life might depend on it.

When he got back to the main hut, Ska was sleeping peacefully beside Arno. Somehow this cheered Tom. If Ska was getting better, then maybe Josh would too.

Harambee! Let's Go!

Thursday, 2am

That night Tom had a nightmare in
which a pride of lions were closing in on him as he
ran down the track to the waterhole. Soon he was
surrounded, cut off, not daring to move. He stood
on the track, the smell strong in his nostrils, his
breath coming in short gasps.

Then he saw that Josh was lying at his feet, still in a
high fever, soaked with sweat. As his brother looked up
at him, Tom could see the lions reflected in the pupils
of his eyes.

Then the pride leapt, their sinewy bodies pouncing

on Tom and, half-asleep, half-awake, he rolled off his straw mattress and bumped into Arno who was curled up beside him.

"What's the matter?" he muttered.

"I was having a dream." Tom was shivering.

"What about?"

"Lions, what else? Josh was lying in their path. I was there too."

"And then?"

"They leapt at me." Tom looked at his watch and saw the time was two am.

"You'd better get some sleep," said Arno. "Kitu will come to collect you before dawn."

"No one told me what time to be ready."

"Well, you need to use your initiative and find out!" Arno replied and turned over.

But Tom was wide awake now and wanted to talk. "Do you think you'll ever get back to your family?"

"As I told you, I can't return to my own country. Not with the present government in charge, anyway," he said sadly, rolling over to face Tom.

"I'm sorry." Tom was ashamed of having taken so little interest in Arno's problems. He wondered what it would be like to know you might never see your family again. It almost seemed beyond his imagination. But if he wanted to see *his* family, to put them out of their misery, he had to be fit enough to run to Osak. Tom thought about the familiar faces of his parents and his eyes filled with tears that he had to blink hurriedly away. "Do I have any chance of passing today's test with Kitu?" he asked anxiously.

Arno didn't reply and his expression was hard to read.

"Or are you going to leave and try and go there without me?" Tom suddenly wondered if Arno's sense of responsibility would make him risk the danger.

But all Arno said was, "I'll give you a day. I said I would."

No longer haunted by nightmares, Tom slept dreamlessly until he was shrugged roughly awake by Kitu. He looked at his watch and groaned. It was only five am and when he staggered to his feet and went outside, the valley was still dark and cold.

Kitu held a bowl of porridge-like mixture in his hands. He gave it to Tom who wolfed it down.

"Run." Kitu said the word in English and smiled at him.

Tom groaned again.

"Run," Kitu repeated and Tom wondered how he'd learnt the word.

"Harambee!" said Tom back to Kitu. Arno had told him it meant "let's do it together" in Swahili. Kitu grinned back at him. He seemed pleased.

Kitu led Tom down a misty track away from the village, starting off slowly and gradually increasing his pace until Tom had the greatest difficulty in keeping up with him. Kitu was wearing a leather bag with a shoulder strap and Tom guessed it contained some food and water. Gradually the distance between them widened and Tom's spirits plunged. What a fool he'd been. Of course, Arno was right. To run like this you did have to have the heart, strength and courage of a lion.

The idea gradually became a fact in Tom's exhausted mind. Kitu had the lion heart. He didn't. And that was what it was all about. He would never make it.

The track had broadened out, but was steep now as they climbed a rolling hillside just as the sun rose, clearing the mist, the strands fleetingly golden. Tom found Kitu was waiting for him, hardly panting.

"Run?" said Kitu, as if the word was a question.

Tom nodded miserably.

After running for what seemed like hours, Tom thought he was going to pass out. His heart was hammering and his chest hurt badly as he gasped for air. The hillside seemed endless, and when they came to what he hoped was the top, it turned out to be a false crest.

Once again Kitu was waiting for him, poised on a rock, ready to run again. He gave Tom what Tom thought might be a disapproving look and then shrugged his shoulders. Kitu had a few beads of sweat on his forehead, but apart from that he seemed to Tom to be as fresh as when he had started running.

"Sorry," Tom managed to get out, his legs like jelly and his tongue cleaving to the roof of his mouth. "I'm very sorry."

"Harambee!" said Kitu with a grin, giving Tom a mock punch on the arm. "Harambee!"

Tom felt his spirits lift. He'd been wrong: Kitu didn't disapprove of him. He liked him.

"Harambee!" He heard Kitu's voice faintly on the air and Tom began to increase his pace. Looking back as they finally arrived at the top of the hill, Tom found he could see for miles. The air was much fresher and he felt cleansed.

Kitu held up a hand and pointed. Dimly, on the far plains in the extreme afternoon heat, Tom saw a shimmering golden glow that when he focused properly became a pride of lions. For a moment Tom wondered if they were real, or if they were some kind of mirage. Then he knew they were real.

The cubs were playing on the grass, making mock attacks on each other while the lionesses lay in the partial shade of some flame trees, stretched out, somnolent but somehow brooding, as if they could jump to their feet at any moment.

The male lions were also lying down, except for one who was swishing his tail and watching the cubs intently, as if to see that their game didn't get out of hand.

Suddenly he reached out with a heavy paw and lightly cuffed one of the cubs who rolled over in the grass with a plaintive cry. The others continued to play and the cub who had just been reprimanded went to rejoin the game, but this time more tentatively.

Oddly, watching the group brought Tom a little comfort. He knew that they were fierce wild animals on their own territory and he and Kitu were running dangerously close to them. But still there was something that was both peaceful and beautiful about the lions' poise and presence.

Tom shook his head and shot a sideways glance at Kitu. Didn't he have any fear? But Tom could see that he did. Kitu's eyes had narrowed, as if he was calculating the chances of their scent being picked up by the lions.

Then Kitu turned to Tom. "Harambee!" he said with an uneasy grin. "Let's go," he added, laughing with pleasure at the opportunity to air the only English phrase he knew.

"Harambee!" said Tom.

Kitu laughed again and then set off at a brisk pace. But this time, from the very outset, Tom found he was able to keep up with Kitu, having to make an effort to do so but not an impossible one. Again Tom felt the thrill of increasing his ability. His feet hardly seemed to touch the ground and his confidence grew. Why, he and Kitu were going so fast now they could even outrun the lions!

Suddenly Tom came down to earth. It was stupid to be unrealistic. He knew the lions couldn't be outrun.

They ran on until Tom saw a group of flame trees that he thought he recognised, and then saw another tree that looked as if it had been hit by lightning. He'd definitely seen this one before, with its blackened, gnarled trunk, and he knew that they were on the way home to Matendu.

Suddenly Tom was shaken by his thoughts. Home was Matendu? What rubbish! Home was Ealing, and what about his parents? And just as importantly, how was Josh's fever?

As he ran, Tom was still amazed. How could he be so distanced from all the people that were so important to him? Now that he was running with Kitu, nothing else seemed to matter any more. In his old life there were so many possessions and activities that he enjoyed. This new life was much more simple, but much more important. He and Kitu were running for their lives. This was the Kala way of graduating into manhood. To run through the territory of the lions. And he was doing that too.

Kitu came to a stop under a tree that held some kind of fruit. Tom thought they might be mangoes and Kitu leapt up and grabbed a couple from the branches. He offered Tom one.

"Thanks," said Tom.

"Asante?" asked Kitu.

"Is that thanks in Swahili?" asked Tom.

"Asante," Kitu repeated, and nodded.

"Asante," said Tom.

Then the two boys lay on their backs and bit into their mangoes. As he did so, Tom suddenly realised he hadn't asked Kitu for any water. But as his lips ran with the juicy fruit of the mango, his thirst suddenly became overpowering – and then was slaked by the juice.

How extraordinary, he thought. How very strange. Why was his thirst so much more under control?

"Harambee!" said Kitu, jumping to his feet.

Tom did the same. "Harambee!" he echoed.

Then, just before they began to run again, Kitu pointed up at the sky.

Tom saw a flock of egrets diving down on some cattle that were grazing nearby. They alighted on the backs of the cattle and Tom remembered that Arno had told him the egrets rode them and ate the ticks right off their hide.

Tom made a pecking motion and Kitu grinned and made the same gesture back. He had understood. A real thrill of joy ran through Tom. He and Kitu were communicating. They were friends.

When Tom and Kitu got back to Matendu, Tom turned and offered him his hand.

"Thanks," he said.

Kitu grinned. "Asante," he said. "Thanks."

"Asante," said Tom, suddenly self-conscious.

Then he waved and headed for the hut where Josh lay. His elation started to fade. He was in a remote tribal village and his brother could be dying.

It was dark in the hut and there was no sign of Arno. Tom went over to the mat and looked down at Josh. His eyes were closed and there was sweat on his forehead, but his body seemed to be slightly less damp.

Could the herbal cure be working?

"Josh?..."

There was an answering mumble.

"It's me, Josh. How do you feel?"

"Lousy. You been on your run?"

"Yes."

"How did you get on?"

"OK. I'm only practising."

"You're not going to join their stupid initiation rites, are you?"

"No. I'm going to try to get to the air strip."

"You? On your own?"

"There's no radio here. And Arno's going to come some of the way with me."

"I want him to stay with me!"

Suddenly they were slipping back to being two squabbling brothers again. But Tom knew he had to comfort Josh.

"I shan't be long."

"What about Arno?"

"He's only coming a little way with me. He'll be back with you again quite quickly."

"OK." Josh tried to sit up, but fell back on to the mattress with a groan. "I want to say something."

"What?"

"Thanks."

"What for?"

"Running for me. I appreciate that."

Tom came nearer. "Asante," he said.

"What's that mean?"

"Thanks in Swahili."

"I don't want to say anything in Swahili," complained Josh. "I just want to get home."

When supper was over, Tom excused himself and went to the hut. He lay down and blissfully closed his eyes. But then he sensed someone standing over him, and turning on to his back, looked up to see Arno.

"I saw Kitu," Arno said. "He said some good things about you. He thinks you can reach Osak."

"That's great!"

"Get some sleep," said Arno. "You've done well. Really well."

Suddenly all his worries disappeared and Tom closed his eyes again with jubilation. He'd made it. Well, almost. He'd won the chance to prove himself.

The Journey Begins

Friday, 5am

Tom woke very early, feeling more deeply refreshed than he could ever remember. Arno was awake beside him, Ska still sleeping peacefully at his side, a new bandage around his wound.

"You're still determined?" whispered Arno.

"You bet I am."

"And you still feel you can reach Osak on your own?"

"Of course."

"I admire you, Tom."

"I know how tough it's going to be. But Kitu showed me how to keep going. How's Josh?"

"His fever's under control. We'll go and see him before we set out."

Josh lay on his straw mattress, his face grey and exhausted in the dim dawn light, looking like a vast, stranded whale. His leg was in a new and less primitive splint which must have been put on last night.

There was a woman sitting beside him, crouched on the floor.

"This is Eya," said Arno. "She is Josh's nurse."

Tom smiled at her, noticing how still and calm she was. He soon saw that Arno had been right and that Josh's fever seemed to have broken.

But his anxiety was as great as ever.

"What's happened?" he asked.

"Nothing," said Tom and he began to speak to his brother as reassuringly as he could. "I'm going to try and reach the air strip at Osak. They'll soon get a helicopter out to you. Arno's coming with me some of the way and then he's coming back to keep an eye on you." Tom realised he'd told Josh all this before, but he hoped the repetition was reassuring.

But Josh didn't find what Tom had said in the least reassuring. "You'll die out there," he muttered. "I know you always have to prove yourself, but this is madness."

"I can do it!"

"Rubbish!"

"I told you last night." Tom was getting indignant. "I went for a training run with Kitu. It gave me stamina, Josh, stamina and confidence. I'll be OK."

"And the lions?"

Eya began to talk to Arno urgently in Swahili.

"Eya says you're not to agitate him," said Arno.

Tom sighed. "I think I've done that already." He turned back to Josh. "I'll see you soon," he said. "Very soon."

Josh simply closed his eyes against the horror of it all. Then he opened them again. "So when are you going?"

"Arno and I are going today. We've got to get you more medical help."

"You're going to risk running through the lions' territory?"

"I'll be OK."

"Why *should* you go? Why can't Arno go instead, or

go all the way there with you? I'll be OK here." Josh was getting more and more agitated.

"Osak's too dangerous for him to go to. It's too close to Uganda and he could put his family in terrible danger. I'm taking a risk, but I have to get there."

"How long will it take you?" There was an edge of panic in Josh's voice.

"I could be gone for a couple of days. But I'll really push on. I'm not going to hang about."

Josh gave a half sob and reached out for Tom's hand. "Don't go," he pleaded. "You might die!"

"I have to."

"They'll come searching for us here now they know we haven't arrived at Kisimu."

"We can't guarantee that – or they might not get here for ages. I don't want you getting any sicker, Josh."

"How can you be sure you'll get to this air strip?"

"I'm determined to get there so we can reach Mum and Dad."

"And then?"

"You'll be rescued." Tom was feeling increasingly troubled by Josh's anxiety. But he had to go; like the Kala boys – he had to prove himself.

"What about the lions, Tom?"

"Stop worrying." Tom gently pressed Josh's hand. "They're much less active in daylight – they're not out hunting. I'll be OK."

"But what am I supposed to do?"

"Get better. They've set your leg and your fever's coming down."

Josh looked at him curiously. "You really believe in the Kala, don't you?"

"Yes – and in our survival," replied Tom firmly.

Eya began to speak in Swahili again and Arno touched Tom's shoulder. "We must go. Now."

"I reckon the distance is about forty miles," said Arno as he and Tom both ran into the early morning mist, taking the same direction that Tom and Kitu had only yesterday. "We'll have to be very careful about the bearing." Arno held the compass in his hand. "We can't just stick to the trails."

"Wait a minute," said Tom. "What's that?"

They could both see a shadowy figure running in the opposite direction.

"Kitu!" Tom suddenly realised who the figure

was. "Kitu—"

The shadow paused, turned and waved.

"Thanks for everything!" yelled Tom. "Asante!"
But Kitu was already running again and was soon lost
in the mist. "He was great," said Tom. "He really
helped me train."

"So let's see how good a job he's done." Arno
grinned at him.

As they jogged on, now in silence, Arno and Tom were
aware of unseen presences all around them. The rustle
of leaves, a snapped branch, the distant cries of hyenas.
But so far at least there was no sound or smell of lions.

In the background were the constant rhythms of
insects, tree frogs and crickets and Tom found himself
thinking constantly of Kitu. It wasn't the same running
without him.

It seemed like they'd been running for ages, the
morning getting hotter and hotter, when the terrain
began to slope gradually downwards. Tom could see a
long depression that was obviously the dried-out bed of
a river. They had taken three bottles of water each in

their rucksacks. Tom also had a small tent and a limited food supply. Arno was to turn back at mid-afternoon, and leave Tom most of the water.

When he reached the river bed, Tom discovered that it was not as dry as he had imagined. The mud at the bottom was still sticky and damp.

"There's been no rain since we came here," he said. "So how come this mud is so damp?"

"There must be another source of water somewhere, or the Kala couldn't farm. A waterhole, maybe."

"Where is it then?"

They eventually found the waterhole, almost hidden, higher up on the hillside. Some drops of water were oozing out of the grass nearby, which was spongy and bog-like. But the water was constantly evaporating in the heat and there wasn't nearly enough to top up even one of the water bottles. Lower down, however, Tom could see that the dried-out river bed circled a clump of pepper trees surrounded by foliage.

'We should be able to get some water down there. The bottles are only half full." Tom was obsessed by the fact that half full was not good enough. Suppose they couldn't get any more for a long while? They would have wasted an opportunity. Suddenly Tom remembered how he had felt when he was running with Kitu. He hadn't needed water then, had he? So why was he worrying now?

Then he noticed something, and turned to Arno: "Look at the grass down there. It's bright green."

"Probably a swamp. The earth could be practically liquid, particularly if the swamp's shaded from the sun."

"I'll go and look." Tom began to run down the hillside.

Arno called after him. "Be careful!"

But Tom hadn't noticed the urgency in his voice. He was too preoccupied with filling up the water bottles. As he ran he thought of Kitu again, missing him badly. Then suddenly Tom realised what he was really afraid of. Being alone.

Swamp

Friday, 12pm

Tom finally reached the swamp. It
was foul-smelling, the grass a sickly green.

"Tom – stop! Get out of there! You could go right under! There's no point getting water from a swamp anyway!" Arno was at least ten metres behind him, inching his way forwards, checking every step he took. He was incredibly slow and Tom grew increasingly impatient with him.

Then Tom heard a distant animal noise and paused, looking round anxiously. The roar came again, much closer this time.

"Lions!" yelled Tom, moving ahead faster.

"Not necessarily. And for God's sake look where you're going!"

"I'm not going to hang around to be eaten alive," said Tom, panicking.

"Don't be such a fool. A lion's not going to try and get across a swamp. They're much heavier than us. They wouldn't stand a chance – and neither will you if you don't get out of there! You need to test the ground, Tom. Be careful!"

Tom slowed down, but he still wasn't looking where he was going, absorbed now by the need to find a place of safety, away from the roaring he felt sure he could still hear.

He pushed on impatiently, seeing bright green grass and only the odd patch of mud.

"Watch out!" Arno warned him again. "Be really careful."

"I'm fine," snapped Tom and moved confidently forward.

The next moment he was up to his knees in thick, black mud.

"Help me," yelled Tom. There was no firm base

beneath his feet, only mud that sucked him further down. He began to struggle furiously, immediately making his plight much worse. Tom had never been so afraid. At least with the lions he had been able to climb a tree to evade them, but now there seemed nothing he could do to save himself.

"Stop struggling!" shouted Arno. "You've got to stop struggling! Try not to move at all."

Despite his panic, Tom stopped and suddenly seemed to become more stable. But he still couldn't find anything firm beneath his feet, only the deadly, sinking mud, and with nothing to grip on to he had the strange sensation that he was dangling in space.

Then, under a distant pepper tree, Tom was sure he could see a moving shadow. "There's something over there!" he yelled. He began to struggle again, sinking deeper until he was almost up to his chest in the filthy, stinking mud.

Arno spoke quietly, trying to calm him. "There's nothing over there," he said. "I promise you." Then he grabbed at a dead vine and lay on his stomach, pushing the vine across the mud to Tom. "Grab this. Then grip hard and I'll try to pull you out."

Tom did as he was told, saying to Arno, "OK. Pull!"

Arno pulled, but nothing happened, and Tom knew that the mud had locked him in tight. Panic filled him again as he tried to push down hard with his legs, but that only seemed to make him sink lower.

"Try and lean forward," shouted Arno.

"I can't."

"*Try again.*" Arno had adopted a steely patience. "Go on – push your chest forward and try to kick out with your legs."

Tom tried and only sank a little deeper, splashing the muddy water round him into the air. Some landed in Tom's mouth, and he coughed and spluttered, spitting it out. Arno's instructions seemed to be fatal; the mud was up to his armpits now.

"It's no good."

"Try to throw yourself forward."

"Arno – I'm sinking deeper. Can't you understand?"

"Be quiet," Arno ordered. "Just be quiet and concentrate. Take a firm grip and let me do the rest."

But as Arno pulled, the vine parted.

*

Tom sank back, realising that Arno had been succeeding, would have succeeded, if only the vine hadn't broken. Now Arno was desperately looking for another but Tom was sure he wouldn't find one in time, that he was going to die by slow, slimy suffocation. It seemed horrifying to die in a bog after everything that had happened to him already. He closed his eyes against his fate.

When Tom opened his eyes again, Arno had returned with another vine, long and thin, which looked hopelessly inadequate. "Grab this! For God's sake, Tom – grab it."

"*Harambee!*" said Kitu in Tom's mind. "*Come on. Let's do it together!*"

"Grab the vine!"

Tom reached out and grabbed it and Arno braced himself, turning his back on Tom, pulling as hard as he could. The vine was certainly thin, but fortunately it was particularly strong.

Suddenly the ooze began to make violent, belching sounds, but Arno paused to take a firmer grip on the vine and immediately Tom began to sink again.

Quickly, Arno began to pull harder, straining every

muscle, desperately hoping the vine would hold. The squelching and belching sounds increased, and to Tom's amazement the mud reluctantly began to give him up. "Keep pulling," he yelled at Arno. "Please keep pulling!"

Suddenly the bog gave an even louder belching sound and Tom began to feel the mud slowly receding, as if some huge monster was gradually losing its grip, reluctantly giving him his freedom. With a last despairing gulp, the bog seemed to spit him out, and Tom was free. He could feel safe, solid ground beneath him. Miraculously even his shoes were still on his feet, and his bag, though covered in mud, still over his shoulder.

For a while Tom just lay there on his face, too exhausted to move. Then he remembered about the lions. But when Tom eventually struggled up, he saw, to his relief, that there were no animals in sight. Then he began to shake.

"Sit down for a bit. You're in shock." Arno was also shaking and gasping for breath.

"I've been a liability."

"No." Arno was only being generous, and Tom felt deeply ashamed.

"Of course I'm a liability." But he hadn't been with

Kitu, had he? Or had he been fooling himself all the time?

"We all need to learn from our mistakes. I've always done that," said Arno gently and without accusation. "I'm like you, Tom. I want to do my own thing."

"You were great." Tom was still ashamed of how stupid he'd been. He got stiffly to his feet and glanced back at the glutinous mud. Thank God Arno had been with him. It was ironic that now Tom trusted him completely, Arno was about to leave him. He would have to cope with the rest of the long journey to Osak alone. But, after all, it was *his* choice to do so, this time – and his choice alone.

Like a Warrior

Tom had never felt such terrible heat before. It clung to him, like a suffocating warm blanket.

"How do you feel?" asked Arno.

"I'm OK."

"This is where we have to part." But Arno seemed undecided. "Walking out on you like this..." he muttered. "What would your parents think?"

"They'd think you had to get back to Josh. He's the one who needs you."

"Come on—"

But Tom interrupted him. "You know what's he's like—"

"He doesn't *have* to be like that. Josh could have much more confidence – if he tried to. And, I suppose, if you don't put him down too much!"

"I'm working on that," said Tom. "But people don't, can't, change overnight."

Arno nodded. "Fair enough. Let's just check you out before I go," he said.

"I've got all I need."

"Compass?"

"Yes."

"The bearing is north-east."

"I've got that."

"Stick to it." Arno still hesitated.

But Tom wanted to get going. "Keep safe on the way back to Matendu – and I'm sorry, Arno."

"About what?"

"Josh and I landed you in this mess."

"So you did. But I'd rather you didn't start apologising again. You've done brilliantly since then."

Tom felt a glow of satisfaction and encouragement.

He looked down at the compass, set the bearing, and began to run.

The worst thing about the next stage of the journey was that there was no shade and the heat was relentless. Under the burning sun the plain stretched before him, beautiful but desolate, with its shrivelled grass and occasional pepper trees. Tom had started off with a couple of full water bottles but he quickly became desperately thirsty and all too soon had already finished off the first, conscious that he had to preserve the second.

Tom struggled on, his body feeling like a lead weight and continuous sweat streaming down his face. His shorts were chafing his legs and despite the factor-50 sun cream he'd applied the back of his neck was starting to feel as if it was sunburnt. He was also beginning to feel feverish. The sweat was streaming down his face, his throat incredibly dry. He felt hot and surprisingly cold by turns, shivering all the time as well as continuing to sweat.

Soon a haze began to form in front of his eyes and once he staggered and fell, grazing his knees.

Despite knowing that he should rest, Tom continued to drive himself on, wiping the sweat out of his eyes, his head full of a ringing sound that soon changed to a low roaring, as if he was being pursued by a pride of lions. He could smell their muscle-bound flanks as they padded beside him. Then he fell again. He couldn't see any lions, but he seemed to have ended up on his back on the scorched grass in the full heat of the blazing sun, unable to move.

For a while he gazed up at the steel grey sky with its blazing white disc, the roaring in his ears sometimes sounding like the noise of lions and at other times like waves on a pebbly shore.

He thought of Josh. Maybe he was dying of a fever – a fever just like his own – but even that couldn't make Tom drag himself to his feet. He lay gazing up at the vast sky, a miserable speck of wretched humanity. He imagined that soon he would roast to death and be reduced to dry, bleached bone.

The roaring came again and the lions stood over him, their victorious eyes gazing down into his. Tom waited for the first attack, the first tearing of his flesh, but nothing happened.

Images of Josh and Ska and Arno repeated and re-repeated in Tom's head, became superimposed on one another and then cleared again. "I'm sorry," he muttered. "I'm sorry, Josh. I should have helped you. Why didn't I help you? Why couldn't I help you?"

Slowly he got to his feet and discovered again that there were no lions, that they had been an illusion. Tom staggered on and then fell, lying on his back again, gazing up at the blazing sun. He closed his eyes and saw the lion looking down at him. Dimly, Tom knew that he must be hallucinating again. As he managed to turn over on to his front the images abruptly disappeared. Instead he only saw darkness – a deep, dark well into which he felt he was plunging.

Then the darkness became a soft pillow and he slept.

When Tom surfaced his head was pounding, but his vision was clearer and he didn't feel so feverish. His throat was parched, however, and all he could think of was water. He reached out for the last water bottle and found it a quarter full. Could he have woken and drunk some? Tom had no idea.

With his last ounce of strength, he brought the

bottle to his lips, moistened them and drank a few drops. Then he screwed on the top again and shakily stood up.

The grasslands seemed to stretch out to eternity. It was still very hot and glancing at his watch Tom saw that the time was just after four-thirty. There was the whisper of a breeze.

But the grass was moving.

Tom blinked and stared ahead. He wasn't hallucinating – not any more – although his head ached horribly, as if someone was at work inside it with a hammer.

The grass was still moving.

Tom smelt the familiar bitter smell.

He froze, not daring to move.

Then the lion rose up and began to move slowly towards him. Behind the lion was another, the lioness, a half-grown lion and a couple of cubs. A pride.

The five of them continued to pad towards him. Slowly the lions moved nearer. Then they came to a halt.

The male lion began to swish his tail, making a sweeping sound in the long grass.

Tom glanced behind him. There was a tree, stunted

and dry, with gnarled wood that looked brittle and could snap at any moment. He stared around him but there was no other cover.

Could he get to the gnarled, dead-looking tree?

Would it support his weight?

Tom knew that lions could climb trees too, but he had to do something. He couldn't just wait until one of the pride pounced. Could he?

Should he run or should he walk as slowly as the approaching lions had done, curious, hungry perhaps, but above all territorial, wondering why he was there?

Tom's mind flashed ahead to what his parents would feel when they got the news that Josh had died of fever and he had been killed by a lion. Still rooted to the spot, trying not to move a muscle, Tom looked back at the lions.

They hadn't moved.

The tail swishing continued.

Apart from that the silence was throttling, terrifying, the sweat running into Tom's eyes in a sticky stream.

A lion heart. The phrase came insistently into his head.

What would Kitu and his friends have done? This

was what they were training for. To be strong and know oneself in a difficult situation.

He remembered how fast he and Kitu had run. Tom also remembered how Kitu had made him run twice as fast as he had *ever* imagined he could.

But Kitu wasn't here. There was no one to pace him, no one to encourage him.

A lion heart. That's what he had to have. But on his own.

Tom suddenly sprang into action, turning, jumping and running as fast as he could – and then trying to move faster. He risked a glance over his shoulder.

The lioness and the group were still watching him. But the male lion was beginning to move in his direction.

With a terrified cry, Tom increased his pace. The grass was shimmering with heat and his legs felt like lead.

He turned again. The lion was nearer.

For a moment Tom thought Kitu was running beside him. He was even sure he could see him. Then the shadowy figure seemed to melt away into the haze.

Tom was on his own.

But wasn't that Kitu by the tree, beckoning to him?

"Lion!" Tom thought he heard him shout.

Something raked across his back. Lightly at first but then the pain slowly intensified. His back was clawed again.

Tom stumbled, but managed to stay on his feet, blindly running on, hearing the thudding of the lion's paws on the hard ground behind him. He staggered again but kept going, the bitter smell getting nearer, encroaching, surrounding him.

Please, God, Tom thought to himself. Please, God, don't let him kill me.

There was a weird chattering sound. Suddenly, Tom slammed into the tree he'd seen before. Automatically he reached up, acting by instinct, not really thinking at all. He grabbed a branch and began to haul himself up, but his sweaty hands slid off the branch and he fell, lying on the ground beneath the tree, waiting for the lion's claws to rake him again and again, deeper each time.

There was a very loud chattering noise in his head now.

Was it just in his head?

But why couldn't he smell lion any more?

"Get it over with!" he yelled. "Just get it over with!"

Then there was a great shadow across his face, blotting out the sun. This had to be the lion. Soon he would feel it tearing his flesh. How much would it hurt? How much would he—

The chattering above his head swelled to a loud roar and a great wind blew through the grasses.

Tom rolled over to see the helicopter coming down, blades whirling, and his relief was so great that everything went black.

When he came to, a man in a cap and a T-shirt marked *PARAMEDIC* was by his side. As he lifted Tom into a sitting position and gave him glorious sips of pure, cold water from a flask, elation filled him for a moment.

"Who are you?" the paramedic asked as he looked at the gashes on Tom's back.

"Tom Trent. We had an accident." An accident that now seemed light years away.

"Tom Trent. At last. We've been looking for you everywhere. We've had helicopters and spotter planes searching for you every day. We got to the wrecked jeep in the end and found your camcorder and video, and checked out the Kala. They gave us some directions – but even then you were hard to find."

"What about my brother?"

"We've already air-lifted him to hospital. And the guide and the dog."

"Is Josh going to live?"

"Yes."

"What about the dog?"

"He'll be OK. But you won't be unless I can get those wounds dealt with."

"Where's the lion?"

"I saw one running away. You had a lucky escape. By those claw marks on your back, he must've nearly got you." The paramedic suddenly grinned at him, as if he had been just as shocked as Tom. "Come on. I'll help you aboard." Tom could hardly believe he was being rescued – that the terrible journey was over and he was still alive.

Reunion

A few hours later the helicopter touched down on the helipad on the roof of the hospital at Kisimu. Tom was rushed to the Emergency Room.

The wounds on his back had become increasingly painful during the flight and his fever had intensified. Hot and cold waves were running through him, and there was a constant pounding in his head. Every time he was shifted, the rawness on Tom's back made him groan. Eventually he lapsed into merciful unconsciousness.

When he resurfaced he found himself lying on a

table in the Emergency Room.

There were a number of doctors and nurses swimming in front of his eyes, looking as if they were figures in a distorted mirror. One of the doctors, a man with what seemed to be a hideously elongated face, leant over him.

"The wounds on your back are quite deep and will need stitches, and we're going to give you pain-killing injections. You've also got a fever. Can you tell us how long you've had this?"

Tom tried to speak but he felt too weak. Then he tried again and after a great struggle whispered, "I fell into a swamp. Maybe I got some of the water down my throat."

"That could be the cause." The doctor's face became even longer, stretching from the floor to the ceiling, and Tom passed out.

When Tom woke again, he was lying in a hospital bed in a private room. A nurse was lifting him to check his wounds. The pain returned and he screwed up his face against it.

"You are on your own because you're infectious," said the nurse, pre-empting his question. "Your brother's doing well, and your parents are here. Are you in much pain?"

"Yes," said Tom, and she gave him an injection. Slowly he drifted into deep sleep.

Tom had lost all sense of time. When his parents came in he was surprised to see them. It was almost as if they were strangers.

"Where have you been?" he whispered.

"We've been here all the time," said his father.

Again Tom drifted into sleep, dreaming of running with Kitu, running faster and faster, heading away from the lion which was closely following them, bounding along, teeth bared in a snarl.

Suddenly Kitu vanished, for a moment Tom felt total despair but then he heard Arno's voice on the wind.

"You have to have the heart of a lion – the heart of a lion—"

Again Tom woke, but this time his head was clear and the pain had receded.

His mother took his hand. "You're getting better," she said. "You're getting stronger every day. The doctors are really pleased with you."

"Lion-hearted," he said to his parents over and over again. "I've got to be lion-hearted. Then it will all be OK." He smiled but neither of his parents understood.

Soon Tom was strong enough to sit by the bed in a chair and then, at his own insistence, he was helped down to Josh's room. As he was taken down by wheelchair he asked his father the answer to a question that had been worrying him.

"Where's Arno? What's happened to him?"

"He went back," replied his father. "It was too dangerous for him to be here."

"So I'll never see him again."

"He left you a video," said his mother. "Just like the one you made that your rescuers picked up from the wreck of the jeep. That was an excellent idea, Tom, by the way."

Tom smiled. He wasn't going to make a big deal about that as he would have done once. Instead he asked, "Where's the video Arno made, then?"

"In Josh's room. He won't be parted from it."

Josh lay in the hospital bed with his broken leg in traction.

"How are you?" Tom asked.

"I'm OK. I'm clear of the fever at last. We can thank the Kala for that. The doctors here said they'd done a good job. I gather you picked up a fever too. I've been really worried about you."

"Thanks, Josh. I was thinking – we used to be good mates when we were younger, didn't we?"

"We could be again," said Josh. "We just lost each other somewhere, that's all."

"Good. So where's that video, then?" asked Tom eagerly.

Josh reached out for the remote control and Arno's face appeared on the TV screen. He was sitting on the edge of the bed in a hotel room. Ska was lying on the floor in front of him with a new bandage on, but the dog looked really well at last.

"OK," said Arno. "We met with an accident and don't let's apportion blame. We also met with lions and I reckon you two guys met up with each other after a long, long time. I'm going back tomorrow. I thought I'd leave you to your parents. After all, I was only your guide. But I did guide you to some new experiences, didn't I? Goodbye – and best of luck. I reckon you've both discovered the importance of being lion-hearted. It's not just the physical skill. It's the courage and commitment that makes a Kala warrior. So if you're ever thinking of getting a job in Kenya – a job that really means something – come and look me up."

"You're the warrior, Tom," said Josh, laughing. "I'm definitely *not*!"

"I wouldn't count on that."

"I counted on you." Josh sat up in bed. "I'm sorry I got on so badly with you before," he said. "And that I blamed you for everything."

"So am I," replied Tom. "I did the same. But we'll work together now."

"Yeah. And I want to say this – you kept going," said Josh. "You didn't give up. You really are lion-hearted."

Tom thought of the lions. He was frightened of them, but awed by their beauty too. Could he manage to work with them in some way in the future? Kenya had really gripped his imagination. The wild, he thought. It's got something important for someone like me.

Deep down, Tom knew he would be back. He would

contact Arno and train to be a guide. It was something worth working for.

But more than anything he looked forward to running again – running with Kitu – now they'd done their initiation rites, they would both be men and warriors, running together over the endless African plain.

If books could kill...

Read about another electrifying encounter with a dangerous predator... the bear!

"Masters knows how to pack a story full of fast-moving incidents, sharply drawn characters and emotional turmoil." *Junior Bookshelf*

ISBN 1 84121 910 X   £4.99

PROLOGUE: Night Visitor

Thursday, 9pm – 8 May, 2003

"So give them a chance," said Jon

Barron to his son Glen. "That's all I'm asking." He went back into the lodge, leaving Glen outside. "Just think about it," he called over his shoulder.

Glen didn't immediately follow his father. Instead he decided to spend some time on his own in the Canadian spring night, not to sulk or look childish, but to give himself some space.

Then he heard the snuffling sound. Where was it coming from? Having felt the need to be on his own, Glen suddenly felt apprehensive. What *was* that noise?

Then he noticed that the dustbin at the end of the long back yard was lying on its side. Much of the contents had spilt. Something was sorting through the rubbish on the ground. Something big. Glen didn't know what to do. Should he call his father, or investigate on his own? Because his father had just criticised him Glen was determined to be independent. There were deer in the forest which came right up to the edge of the village where they were staying, as well as elk. So Glen didn't feel particularly afraid now – just a little tense, and certainly curious.

Glen also knew that there were grizzlies and black bears in the forest because that was why his father had travelled to Canada. But of course the scavenger couldn't be a bear. Bears would hardly ever come near civilisation. They were rare and frightened of human beings. He comforted himself with that reassuring thought.

Quietly, Glen approached the dustbin and to his relief the scavenger backed away. It *must* be a deer, he thought. They were nervous creatures, as nervous as he had been just a few moments ago. But now Glen felt much more relaxed, which was more than the deer felt. If it was a deer.

All Glen could see was a shadow, but there was something wrong with the shape of the shadow. Maybe it's a dog, he thought, although a voice in his mind was starting to tell him the shadow was far too big to be a dog.

There was a low growl and Glen froze, his mouth dry and sweat breaking out on his forehead. He felt as if there was something crawling on his skin.

Suddenly the creature stood up on its hind legs and Glen's mind refused to focus. The sweat was running into his eyes now and he felt a weird sensation in his stomach he'd never experienced before – a kind of deadly cold chill.

He was looking at a bear. Not a huge bear, but a bear all the same. Then Glen's mind clicked back into focus and he registered the black hair and the animal's large paws in the wan moonlight.

Glen didn't wait to check out the bear any longer, whatever its size. He turned and ran back towards the lodge, sure he was being pursued and that at any moment he would be thrown to the ground and ripped to pieces.

Glen hurled himself into the welcoming light of the

kitchen to find his father brewing coffee, and the others sitting in the living room watching TV.

"There's a bear out there," he gasped. "A black bear." Suddenly he felt as if he was going to throw up. But to Glen's fury, his warning was greeted with derisive hoots of laughter.

PREDATOR

Got the guts for some Grizzly Action?

Read the rest of *Deathtrap*
to find out what happens next!

Are you ready to face White Death?

**A fin zigzags through the water.
Jack knows it's a shark attack.**

Someone's going to get eaten alive. But there's
one fatal difference. This is no movie. No video
game. It's all for real – and Jack's the victim…

ISBN 1 84121 906 1   £4.99

Will you outrun the Wolf Pack?

**A hungry wolf waits for the thrill
of the kill. Luke knows the score.**

Soon the hunted will be a blood trail. It could
be cool TV. But this isn't a survival game show.
It's all happening in real time. And Luke's
playing for the big prize – his life.

ANTHONY MASTERS

ISBN 1 84121 904 5   £4.99

More Orchard Red Apples

Predator

❑ Shark Attack	Anthony Masters	1 84121 906 1	£4.99
❑ Deathtrap	Anthony Masters	1 84121 910 X	£4.99
❑ Hunted	Anthony Masters	1 84121 904 5	£4.99

Danger

| ❑ Aftershock! | Tony Bradman | 1 84121 552 X | £3.99 |
| ❑ Hurricane! | Tony Bradman | 1 84121 588 0 | £3.99 |

Jiggy McCue Stories

❑ The Poltergoose	Michael Lawrence	1 86039 836 7	£4.99
❑ The Killer Underpants	Michael Lawrence	1 84121 713 1	£4.99
❑ The Toilet of Doom	Michael Lawrence	1 84121 752 2	£4.99
❑ Maggot Pie	Michael Lawrence	1 84121 756 5	£4.99

| ❑ The Fire Within | Chris d'Lacey | 1 84121 533 3 | £4.99 |
| ❑ The Salt Pirates of Skegness | Chris d'Lacey | 1 84121 539 2 | £4.99 |

Orchard Red Apples are available from all good bookshops,
or can be ordered direct from the publisher:
Orchard Books, PO BOX 29, Douglas IM99 1BQ
Credit card orders please telephone 01624 836000 or fax 01624 837033
or e-mail: bookshop@enterprise.net for details.

To order please quote title, author and ISBN
and your full name and address.
Cheques and postal orders should be made payable to 'Bookpost plc.'
Postage and packing is FREE within the UK
(overseas customers should add £1.00 per book).

Prices and availability are subject to change